The Phantom of the Opera

歌劇魅影

Original Author   Gaston Leroux
Adaptors   Louise Benette / David Hwang
Illustrator   Christian Bernardini

WORDS
800

MP3

Let's Enjoy Masterpieces!

All the beautiful fairy tales and masterpieces that you have encountered during your childhood remain as warm memories in your adulthood. This time, let's indulge in the world of masterpieces through English. You can enjoy the depth and beauty of original works, which you can't enjoy through Chinese translations.

The stories are easy for you to understand because of your familiarity with them. When you enjoy reading, your ability to understand English will also rapidly improve.

This series of **Let's Enjoy Masterpieces** are a special reading comprehension booster program, devised to improve reading comprehension for beginners whose command of English is not satisfactory, or who are elementary, middle, and high school students. With this program, you can enjoy reading masterpieces in English with fun and efficiency.

This carefully planned program is composed of 5 levels, from the beginner level of 350 words to the intermediate and advanced levels of 1,000 words. With this program's level-by-level system, you are able to read famous texts in English and to savor the true pleasure of the world's language.

The program is well conceived, composed of reader-friendly explanations of English expressions and grammar, quizzes to help the student learn vocabulary and understand the meaning of the texts, and fabulous illustrations that adorn every page. In addition, with our "Guide to Listening," not only is reading comprehension enhanced but also listening comprehension skills are highlighted.

In the audio recording of the book, texts are vividly read by professional American voice actors. The texts are rewritten, according to the levels of the readers by an expert editorial staff of native speakers, on the basis of standard American English with the ministry of education recommended vocabulary. Therefore, it will be of great help even for all the students that want to learn English.

Please indulge yourself in the fun of reading and listening to English through Let's Enjoy Masterpieces.

卡斯頓·
勒胡

Gaston
Leroux
(1868–1927)

In 1868, Gaston Leroux, a French novelist, was born in Paris, as the son of a wealthy family. After Leroux received his law degree from university, he squandered a considerable inheritance on drinking and gambling. As he ran through his fortune, Leroux began to work as a newspaper correspondent. In the 1890's, as a correspondent, he traveled worldwide. He reported for French papers on the events and exciting adventures across the globe, including the 1905 Russian Revolution.

From the early 1900's, Leroux began to devote himself entirely to writing. He mostly wrote detective novels. After his first success with *The Mystery of the Yellow Room*, starring an amateur detective, Leroux began to gain fame as a writer.

Using his inimitable journalistic writing style, Gaston Leroux wrote many novels that were based on his experiences as a reporter. His novels worked out with such an impeccable sense of logic that readers could feel as if they were part of the actual action and were solving puzzling mysteries themselves. *The Phantom of the Opera* is one of the best-known examples. It earned for Gaston Leroux the reputation of being the greatest French detective novelist of his time. After his death, it was adapted in many stage productions and films. *The Phantom of the Opera* has become an international success.

The Phantom of the Opera is set in the Paris Opera House, where rumors are rampant that there is a ghost causing a series of terrifying incidents. The phantom, Erik, has a scarred face that is hidden behind a mask. He lives in his lair within the catacombs beneath the Paris Opera House. Erik falls in love with a beautiful opera singer, Christine, and he teaches her to sing.

Then one day, Raoul, Christine's childhood sweetheart appears. Erik becomes terribly jealous. During the opening night of an opera, he kidnaps Christine and takes her through the catacombs to an underground lake. At the risk of his life, Raoul enters the cellars to come to her rescue. Despite her love for Raoul, Christine still shows compassion toward the phantom, even after she discovered his horrifically disfigured face. The Phantom of the Opera becomes redeemed by a kiss from Christine.

Finally, the phantom lets Christine and Raoul go free, and then he disappears because he knows his love for Christine cannot be realized.

As seen in *The Beauty and the Beast*, *Hunchback of Notre Dame*, and *King Kong*, the story of heart-rending love between a beautiful female character and a hideous male is a well-known theme in western literature. In the Phantom's love story, the author's accurate, realistic, suspenseful description has all the elements of a successful detective novel and has won the hearts and minds of the readers. In the 21st Century, *The Phantom of the Opera* has become loved all around the world and has had a diversity of creative adaptations in the various artistic media.

HOW TO USE THIS BOOK
本書使用說明

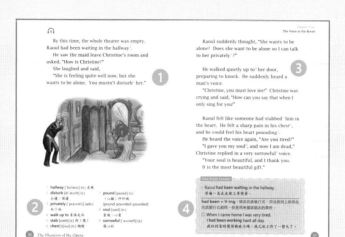

① Original English texts

It is easy to understand the meaning of the text, because the text is rewritten according to the levels of the readers.

② Explanation of the vocabulary

The words and expressions that include vocabulary above the elementary level are clearly defined.

③ Response notes

Spaces are included in the book so you can take notes about what you don't understand or what you want to remember.

④ One point lesson

In-depth analyses of major grammar points and expressions help you to understand sentences with difficult grammar.

🎧 Audio Recording

In the audio recording, native speakers narrate the texts in standard American English. By combining the written words and the audio recording, you can listen to English with great ease.

Audio books have been popular in Britain and America for many decades. They allow the listener to experience the proper word pronunciation and sentence intonation that add important meaning and drama to spoken English. Students will benefit from listening to the recording twenty or more times.

After you are familiar with the text and recording, listen once more with your eyes closed to check your listening comprehension. Finally, after you can listen with your eyes closed and understand every word and every sentence, you are then ready to mimic the native speaker.

Then you should make a recording by reading the text yourself. Then play both recordings to compare your oral skills with those of a native speaker.

How to Improve Reading Ability

如何增進英文閱讀能力

1 Catch key words

Read the key words in the sentences and practice catching the gist of the meaning of the sentence. You might question how working with a few important words could enhance your reading ability. However, it's quite effective. If you continue to use this method, you will find out that the key words and your knowledge of people and situations enables you to understand the sentence.

2 Divide long sentences

Read in chunks of meaning, dividing sentences into meaningful chunks of information. In the book, chunks are arranged in sentences according to meaning. If you consider the sentences backwards or grammatically, your reading speed will be slow and you will find it difficult to listen to English.

You are ready to move to a more sophisticated level of comprehension when you find that narrowly focusing on chunks is irritating. Instead of considering the chunks, you will make it a habit to read the sentence from the beginning to the end to figure out the meaning of the whole.

❸ Make inferences and assumptions

Making inferences and assumptions are part of your ability. If you don't know, try to guess the meaning of the words. Although you don't know all the words in context, don't go straight to the dictionary. Developing an ability to make inferences in the context is important.

The first way to figure out the meaning of a word is from its context. If you cannot make head or tail out of the meaning of a word, look at what comes before or after it. Ask yourself what can happen in such a situation. Make your best guess as to the word's meaning. Then check the explanations of the word in the book or look up the word in a dictionary.

❹ Read a lot and reread the same book many times

There is no shortcut to mastering English. Only if you do a lot of reading will you make your way to the summit. Read fun and easy books with an average of less than one new word per page. Try to immerse yourself in English as often as you can.

Spend time "swimming" in English. Language learning research has shown that immersing yourself in English will help you improve your English, even though you may not be aware of what you're learning.

CONTENTS

Before You Read

Erik (the Ghost)

I was born with a very ugly face. No one can look at me with love, not even my own mother. Even though my face is very ugly, I have a beautiful voice and I am very smart. I built the Opera House, with its many secret doors and passageways. Most people at the Opera House think I am a ghost.

Christine

I am a singer at the Opera House. My voice was not great, so I was an average singer. One night, Erik came to me and has helped me to improve my own voice. However, Erik wants me to love him, and I cannot. I love another man.

Raoul

I am a young man who is about to join the French Navy. When I was young, I was in love with Christine. However, I lost contact with her. One night in Paris, I saw her again as she sang at the Opera House. During this story I find out what happened to her and that she really does still love me!

The Persian

I used to be a policeman in Persia. I have known Erik for a long time. I feel sorry for him, but I know he can be very dangerous. So I live in Paris and keep an eye on Erik.

Chapter One

⓵ The Opera Ghost[1]

Sorelli, one of the most important dancers at the Opera, sat in her dressing room[2]. She was getting ready for[3] the gala[4] performance[5] for the two retiring[6] managers[7] of the Opera. She was enjoying the peace and quiet, but was suddenly interrupted[8] when a group of young girls came running into her room.

The girls were talking excitedly[9].

1. **ghost** [ɡoʊst] (n.)
   鬼魂；幽靈
2. **dressing room**
   化妝室；更衣室
3. **get ready for** 準備好……
4. **gala** [ˋɡeɪlə] (n.)
   慶祝；盛典
5. **performance**
   [pərˋfɔːrməns]
   (n.) 演出；表演

6. **retiring** [rɪˋtaɪərɪŋ]
   (a.) 退休的
7. **manager** [ˋmænɪdʒər]
   (n.) 經理
8. **interrupt** [ˌɪntəˋrʌpt]
   (v.) 打斷；阻礙
9. **excitedly** [ɪkˋsaɪtɪd]
   (adv.) 興奮地；激動地

"The Ghost! We've seen him!" one of them cried out. "We've seen the ghost!"

Sorelli was very superstitious[10].

She was easily frightened[11] by stories of the ghost, but she tried to be brave.

"That's ridiculous[12]!" she told the girls. "You are just being foolish."

"No, no! It's true. We really all saw him," the girls cried out. The chorus[13] girls all claimed[14] to have seen him. In fact[15], whenever anything unfortunate[16] happened in the building, the girls always said, "It was the ghost!"

10. **superstitious** [ˌsuːpərˈstɪʃəs] (a.) 迷信的

11. **frightened** [ˈfraɪtnd] (a.) 驚恐的

12. **ridiculous** [rɪˈdɪkjələs] (a.) 荒謬的；可笑的

13. **chorus** [ˈkɔːrəs] (n.) 合唱團

14. **claim** [kleɪm] (v.) 聲稱；斷言

15. **in fact** 實際上；的確

16. **unfortunate** [ʌnˈfɔːrtʃənət] (a.) 不幸的

For a while[1], many didn't believe the girls. Some thought it was just their crazy imaginations[2].

However, this changed when Joseph Buquet, one of the scene-shifters[3], said, "I saw the most terrible thing in the corridor[4]. It was a figure[5] wearing a dress-suit[6]. At first, I thought he was from the audience[7]. Then, I looked at him more closely[8]. It had no face — it was a skull[9]! The skin was yellow, the eyes were black holes, and the whole figure was terribly thin."

Joseph was a very reliable[10] man, so no one doubted[11] him.

1. **for a while**
   一會兒；一段時間
2. **imagination**
   [ɪˌmædʒəˈneɪʃn] (n.) 想像力
3. **scene-shifter** 換布景的人
4. **corridor** [ˈkɔːrədər] (n.)
   走廊；通道
5. **figure** [ˈfɪgjər] (n.)
   人影；人形
6. **dress-suit** 大禮服
7. **audience** [ˈɔːdiəns] (n.)
   觀眾
8. **closely** [ˈkloʊsli] (adv.)
   接近地；仔細地
9. **skull** [skʌl] (n.) 頭顱
10. **reliable** [rɪˈlaɪəbl] (a.)
    可信賴的；可靠的
11. **doubt** [daʊt] (v.) 懷疑
12. **fireman** [ˈfaɪərmən] (n.)
    火夫；救火者
13. **cellar** [ˈselə(r)] (n.) 地窖
14. **horrifying** [ˈhɑrəfaɪ-ɪŋ] (a.)
    令人恐懼的
15. **clear** [klɪr] (a.)
    清晰的；明顯的
16. **distinctly** [dɪˈstɪŋktɪvli]
    (adv.) 清楚地；確實地

Soon everyone at the Opera began to see strange things. One of the firemen[12], Pampin, said, "I went down into the cellars[13] yesterday morning. When I was down there, I saw the most horrifying[14] thing. I saw a head of fire coming toward me! It was so clear[15]. I remember it very distinctly[16]. It had a head of fire, but the head had no body at all!"

🎧 3

In Sorelli's dressing room, the girls continued their story. "We really saw him!" one of the girls insisted[1]. "It was the ghost!"

Sorelli's dressing room became deathly[2] quiet. All that could be heard was the breathing[3] of the frightened girls. One of the girls put her ear to the wall to try to hear any noise from outside. Her face turned white.

1. **insist** [ɪnˋsɪst]
   (v.) 堅持；堅決認為
2. **deathly** [ˋdɛθli]
   (adv.) 很；似死地
3. **breathing** [ˋbriːðɪŋ]
   (n.) 呼吸

4. **whisper** [ˋwɪspə(r)]
   (v.) 低語；耳語
5. **rustling** [ˋrʌslɪŋ]
   (a.) 沙沙作響的
6. **keep** [kiːp] (v.) 擁有；保留

"Listen!" she whispered[4] in a terrified voice. There was a rustling[5] sound outside the door. Then, suddenly, it stopped.

Sorelli slowly walked to the door and called out, "Who . . . who . . . is there?" There was no answer. "Is there anyone at my door?"

"There is. There is," said Meg, one of the girls. "We all heard the noise. But don't open the door. He can come in if you open the door."

Sorelli did not listen to her.

Sorelli always kept[6] a knife with her and she now took this out from her ankle[7] sheath[8]. She held it in one hand while she cautiously[9] opened the door. All of the chorus girls had gathered[10] into a corner of the room. Sorelli looked in the corridor, but she saw nothing. "There is nothing there," she told the girls.

7. **ankle** [ˋæŋkl] (n.) 足踝
8. **sheath** [ʃiːθ] (n.) (刀劍的) 鞘
9. **cautiously** [ˋkɔːʃəsli]
   (adv.) 小心地；謹慎地
10. **gather** [ˋgæðə(r)] (v.) 聚集

Sorelli, trying to be brave, said, "Calm down[1] girls. No one has seen a ghost."

"But we did see him. And Gabriel saw him, too," another girl added[2].

"Gabriel, the chorus-master[3]?" asked Sorelli. "What did he say?"

"He was in the stage manager's[4] office when that strange Persian[5] man . . . you know the one, came into the room . . ."

"Yes," said Sorelli, "I know the Persian." Everyone at the Opera House knew the Persian. The girls were afraid of him.

1. **calm down**
   冷靜；鎮定下來
2. **add** [æd] (v.) 補充說道
3. **chorus-master** 合唱團長
4. **stage manager** 舞台監督
5. **Persian** [`pɜːʃən] (n.)
   波斯人
6. **rush** [rʌʃ] (v.) 衝；奔

7. **slip** [slɪp] (v.) 滑跤；失足
8. **stairwell** [`sterwel] (n.)
   樓梯間
9. **bruise** [bruːz] (n.)
   淤傷；傷痕
10. **describe** [dɪ`skraɪb] (v.)
    描繪；敘述

"So what happened?" Sorelli asked.

"As soon as he saw the Persian, Gabriel became crazy and he rushed[6] out of the office.

Unfortunately, he slipped[7] in the stairwell[8] and fell all the way down the stairs. Mother and I found him at the bottom of the stairs. He was covered with blood and bruises[9]. He finally told us why he was so frightened. You see, he had looked over the Persian's shoulder, and he saw the ghost standing behind him!

Gabriel was terrified!"

"What did the ghost look like?" Sorelli wanted to know.

"He was wearing a dress-suit, just like Joseph Buquet described[10] him. And his head was like a skull!" the girl said.

One Point Lesson

◆ Sorelli, **trying to be brave**, said, "Calm down girls. No one has seen a ghost."
莎蕾莉，試著鼓起勇氣，說道：「冷靜點，女孩們！沒有人見過什麼幽靈的。」

分詞構句：trying to be brave 的主詞與 said 的主詞相同，故省略主詞，將動詞改為現在分詞的形式。

e.g. **Folding arms**, he was sitting alone.
他環抱著雙臂，獨自站著。

21

"My mother says Joseph Buquet shouldn't talk so much," Meg said quietly.

Meg's mother, Madame Giry, also worked at the Opera as a box keeper[1].

"What did your mother tell you?" the girls asked Meg.

"She said the ghost didn't like people talking about him," Meg replied slowly. "It's because of Box 5. Mom's in charge of[2] Box 5, you see. Box 5 is the ghost's box," she told them. "That's where he goes during performances.

No one else can go there."

"Has your mother seen him, then?" the girls asked.

1. **box keeper** 包廂管理人
2. **in charge of** 負責；主管
3. **skeleton** [`skelɪtn] (n.) 骸骨；骨骼
4. **nonsense** [`nɑːnsns] (n.) 胡說；廢話
5. **program** [`prougræm] (n.) 節目表
6. **make sense of** 理解；有意義

"No," Meg explained, "you can't see him.
All that talk about his dress-suit, and the
skeleton[3], and the head of fire, is all just
nonsense[4]. Mother's never seen him.
She just hears him when he's in the box.
She also gives him his program[5]."

The girls looked at each other. They could
not make sense of[6] Meg's story at all.

Suddenly, the dressing-room door opened, and a woman came rushing in. Her eyes were wide open[1], and full of terror[2]. "Joseph Buquet!" she gasped[3]. "He's dead. Someone found his body[4] in the cellar. He was hanged[5]!"

1. **wide open** 張得很開
2. **terror** [ˋterə(r)] (n.) 恐懼
3. **gasp** [gæsp] (v.) 喘著氣說
4. **body** [ˋbɑːdi] (n.) 屍體
5. **hang** [hæŋ] (v.) 吊死；絞死
6. **shocked** [ʃɑːkt] (a.) 震驚的
7. **blurt out** 脫口說出
8. **take back** 收回
9. **investigation** [ˌɪnvestɪˋgeɪʃn] (n.) 調查
10. **suicide** [ˋsjuːɪˌsaɪd] (n.) 自殺
11. **rope** [roup] (n.) 繩；索

The room was full of shocked[6] faces.

"The ghost did it," Meg blurted out[7]. She then quickly covered her mouth trying to take back[8] her words. She feared the ghost might hurt her, too. "I didn't say that," she said. "I didn't say anything at all."

But other people agreed with her.

"Yes, it must have been the ghost."

Later, there was an investigation[9].

However, it was decided that it was "natural suicide[10]." Then the strangest thing happened. The rope[11] by which Joseph was hanged suddenly disappeared[12]!

The managers said, "Somebody must have taken it for a souvenir[13]. We will find out what happened to it eventually[14]."

12. **disappear** [ˌdɪsəˈpɪr] (v.)
    消失；不見
13. **souvenir** [ˌsuːvəˈnɪr] (n.)
    紀念品
14. **eventually** [ɪˈventʃuəli]
    (adv.) 最後；終於

A   True or False.

T F   ① Joseph Buquet insisted he saw the opera ghost in the corridor.

T F   ② Sorelli could find the ghost out of her dressing room.

T F   ③ Everyone believed Joseph Buquet committed suicide.

B   Combine the given sentences with proper relative pronouns.

Sorelli was a dancer. She danced at the Opera.
⇨ Sorelli was a dancer **who** danced at the Opera.

① Meg's mother is the woman. She is in charge of Box 5.

⇨ _____

② Joseph Buquet was the man. His body was found in the cellar.

⇨ _____

③ He saw a head of fire. It had no body.

⇨ _____

C Choose the correct answer.

1 What did Sorelli believe about ghosts?

    (a) She believed that they didn't exist at all.

    (b) She was very superstitious and was scared of ghost stories.

    (c) She thought ghosts were not frightening.

2 What does Meg's mother do for the ghost?

    (a) She makes him a cup of tea.

    (b) She gives him his brochure.

    (c) All of the above.

D Fill in the blanks with the given words. Remember to change the form of the verbs.

| rush | be covered | frightened | find | fall | slip |

"As soon as he saw the Persian, Gabriel became crazy and he **1** _____ out of the office. Unfortunately, he **2** _____ in the stairwell and **3** _____ all the way down the stairs. Mother and I **4** _____ him at the bottom of the stairs. He **5** _____ with blood and bruises. He finally told us why he was so **6** _____. You see, he had looked over the Persian's shoulder, and he saw the ghost standing behind him!

The Paris Opera House

Gaston Leroux's story is set in the world-famous Paris Opera House. Many of Leroux's readers thought that such a building with its huge stage, famous chandelier, secret underground passages, and even an underground lake could not exist. However, the Paris Opera House actually has all these features!

There are seats for more than 2,000 people. In the back wall of the theater there are "boxes" on each floor. Leroux chose Box 5, which really does exist, as the Phantom's private seat because it is near the exit.

A massive chandelier does hang over the theater, and in 1896, it fell during a performance. It killed the person sitting in seat 13, and many people think this event inspired Leroux to write his novel.

There is also a lake under the House, which is used as "ballast" for the weight of the stage. However, this lake is not very large, and there is no island in the middle where the Phantom has his house! Perhaps this is the only feature of Leroux's story that does not correspond to the actual Opera House in Paris.

Chapter Two

The Voice in the Room

The gala performance that evening was a complete[1] triumph[2]. It was truly the most successful performance ever held in[3] the Opera.

Members of the audience continually[4] called out for an encore[5]. All of the dancers, composers[6] and singers had worked in perfect harmony to produce such superb[7] performances.

1. **complete** [kəm`pliːt] (a.)
   徹底的；完全的
2. **triumph** [`traɪʌmf] (n.) 勝利
3. **be held in . . .** 在……舉行
4. **continually** [kən`tɪnjuəli]
   (adv.) 不斷地；不絕地
5. **encore** [`ɑːŋkɔː(r)] (n.) 安可
6. **composer** [kəm`pouzə(r)]
   (n.) 作曲家
7. **superb** [suː`pɜːrb] (a.)
   極佳的；一流的
8. **outshine** [ˌaut`ʃaɪn] (v.)
   勝過；比……更優秀
9. **in full bloom** 盛開
10. **intensity** [ɪn`tensəti] (n.)
    熱烈；強烈
11. **moved** [muːvd] (a.)
    被感動的
12. **trio** [`triːou] (n.)
    三重唱（奏）曲
13. **Faust**
    歌德的作品《浮士德》
14. **go wild** 變得瘋狂、熱烈
15. **faint** [feɪnt] (v.) 昏倒
16. **carry** [`kæri] (v.) 搬；運送

But no performance outshone[8] Christine Daae's. She had never been the best singer but tonight she was like a flower in full bloom[9], singing with great passion and intensity[10].

All in the audience were deeply moved[11] during her performance in the prison scene and the final trio[12] in *Faust*[13].

At the end of her performance, the audience went wild[14]. However, Christine, having put all of her heart and soul into her singing, fainted[15] and had to be carried[16] to her dressing room.

🎧 8

There was one man
in the audience who
listened to Christine Daae
with special intensity.
This was the young Viscount[1] Raoul Chagny.
He had come to the performance with his
older brother, the Count[2] Philippe Chagny.

1. **viscount** [`vaɪkaunt] (n.)
   子爵（大寫）
2. **count** [kaunt]
   (n.) 伯爵（大寫）
3. **well-balanced**
   神智健全的；平衡的
4. **widow** [`wɪdou] (n.) 寡婦
5. **naval** [`neɪvəl] (a.) 海軍的

Philippe, 41, had raised his much younger brother with his sister and an aunt after their parents had died. Philippe was very proud of his brother, Raoul. Raoul had grown into a successful, well-balanced[3], young man.

From his aunt, the widow[4] of a naval[5] officer[6], he had developed a love for the sea. He was very soon to begin a career[7] in the navy[8].

While[9] Raoul still had some time in Paris, Philippe had decided to introduce him to some artistic delights[10] in the city.
The opera was one of them.

That evening, during the performance, Raoul said to his brother, "She looks ill, like she's going to faint. She's never sung like that before. I must go and see her."

6. **officer** [ˋɔːfɪsə(r)] (n.) 軍官
7. **career** [kəˋrɪr] (n.) 職業
8. **navy** [ˋneɪvi] (n.)
   海軍；艦隊
9. **while** [waɪl] (conj.)
   當……的時候
10. **delight** [dɪˋlaɪt] (n.)
    樂事；樂趣

Raoul entered her room just when the theater doctor did. Christine had only just regained[1] consciousness[2] and Raoul said, "Doctor, wouldn't it be better if everyone left the room?"

"Yes," agreed the doctor. "Everyone out! I want everyone out!" shouted the doctor. Raoul, the doctor, the maid[3] and Christine were the only ones left in the room.

When Christine saw Raoul, she asked, "Sir, who are you?"

Raoul replied, "Christine, I am the boy who long ago rescued[4] your scarf[5] from the sea."

Christine looked at the doctor and the maid and they all laughed. Raoul felt very insulted[6] and said, "If you do not remember me, then I would like to speak to you in private[7]."

1. **regain** [rɪ`geɪn] (v.) 恢復
2. **consciousness**
   [`kɑːnʃəsnəs] (n.)
   意識；知覺
3. **maid** [meɪd] (n.)
   女僕；侍女
4. **rescue** [`reskjuː] (v.)
   搭救；援救
5. **scarf** [skɑːrf] (n.) 圍巾
6. **insult** [ɪn`sʌlt] (v.)
   侮辱；羞辱
7. **in private** 私下
8. **restless** [`restləs] (a.)
   得不到休息的

"Come back when I am better," Christine said. "Please, all of you go. I am restless[8] this evening."

By this time, the whole theater was empty. Raoul had been waiting in the hallway[1].

He saw the maid leave Christine's room and asked, "How is Christine?"

She laughed and said, "She is feeling quite well now, but she wants to be alone. You mustn't disturb[2] her."

1. **hallway** [ˋhɔːlweɪ] (n.) 走廊
2. **disturb** [dɪˋstɜːrb] (v.)
   打擾；煩擾
3. **privately** [ˋpraɪvətli] (adv.)
   私下地
4. **walk up to** 直接走向
5. **stab** [stæb] (v.) 刺（傷）
6. **chest** [tʃest] (n.) 胸膛

7. **pound** [paʊnd] (v.)
   （心臟）怦怦跳
   (pound-pounded-pounded)
8. **soul** [soʊl] (n.)
   靈魂；心靈
9. **sorrowful** [ˋsɑːrəufl] (a.)
   傷心的

Raoul suddenly thought, "She wants to be alone? Does she want to be alone so I can talk to her privately[3]?"

He walked quietly up to[4] her door, preparing to knock. He suddenly heard a man's voice.

"Christine, you must love me!" Christine was crying and said, "How can you say that when I only sing for you!"

Raoul felt like someone had stabbed[5] him in the heart. He felt a sharp pain in his chest[6], and he could feel his heart pounding[7].

He heard the voice again, "Are you tired?"

"I gave you my soul[8], and now I am dead," Christine replied in a very sorrowful[9] voice.

"Your soul is beautiful, and I thank you. It is the most beautiful gift."

One Point Lesson

◆ Raoul **had been waiting** in the hallway.
勞爾一直在走廊上等待著。

---

had been + V-ing：過去完成進行式，用法原則上與現在完成進行式相同，但是用來描述過去的事件。

e.g. When I came home I was very tired.
I had been working hard all day.
我回到家時覺得精疲力竭，我已經工作了一整天了。

Now Raoul decided to wait in a dark corner[1].

He felt so many emotions[2], but especially he felt love for Christine and hate for the unknown[3] man.

"I want to know who it is I hate," he thought.

Soon after, Christine left her room, leaving[4] the door unlocked[5]. As soon as she was gone, Raoul went into her room and shut[6] the door.

It was completely dark.

"Who are you?" he called out. "Where are you hiding[7]? Come out now coward[8]!"

He lit[9] a match[10] to light the gas lights[11].

He looked all through the room but found nothing. It was a complete[12] mystery[13]!

"A secret passageway[14]?" he thought to himself. "Or am I going mad[15]!"

1. **corner** [ˈkɔːrnə(r)] (n.) 角落
2. **emotion** [ɪˈmoʊʃn] (n.) 感情；情感
3. **unknown** [ˌʌnˈnoʊn] (a.) 陌生的；未知的
4. **leave** [liːv] (v.) 使……保持某種狀態
5. **unlocked** [ˌʌnˈlɑːkt] (a.) 沒有鎖的
6. **shut** [ʃʌt] (v.) 關上；關緊

7. **hide** [haɪd] (v.) 躲藏
8. **coward** [`kaʊərd] (n.) 懦夫
9. **light** [laɪt] (v.) 點火；點亮
   (light-lit-lit)
10. **match** [mætʃ] (n.) 火柴
11. **gas light** 煤氣燈光
12. **complete** [kəm`pliːt] (a.)
   完全的

13. **mystery** [`mɪstri] (n.)
   神秘的事物；秘密
14. **passageway** [`pæsɪdʒweɪ]
   (n.) 走廊；通道
15. **go mad**
   發瘋；失去理智

Later that night, there was a dinner for the two retiring managers of the theater.

Everyone was enjoying the meal[1] when suddenly, a strange figure[2] appeared[3]. He was wearing a suit and his face looked like a skull.

"It's the Opera ghost!" people whispered. "It's the Phantom[4] of the Opera."

The strange figure said loudly, "Joseph Buquet's death was not a suicide."

Everyone, especially the managers, were completely stunned[5]. The figure suddenly disappeared from the room.

1. **meal** [mi:l] (n.) 一餐
2. **figure** [`fɪgjər] (n.) 人影;人形
3. **appear** [ə`pɪr] (v.) 出現
4. **phantom** [`fæntəm] (n.) 幽靈;幻影
5. **stunned** [stʌnd] (a.) 震驚的;目瞪口呆的
6. **joke** [dʒouk] (n.) 玩笑;戲謔
7. **ex-** 〔字首〕以前的
8. **document** [`dɑ:kjumənt] (n.) 文件
9. **read** [ri:d] (v.) 寫著;讀起來
10. **franc** [fræŋk] (n.) 法郎(法國的貨幣單位)
11. **available** [ə`veɪləbl] (a.) 可利用的;可得到的

Sometime after, the two retired managers were sitting down talking to the two new managers, Richard and Moncharmin.

"We've helped you all we can," they said. "We just need to talk about this Opera ghost."

Manager Richard laughed and thought, "It's all a joke[6]." But he asked, "What does it want?"

One of the ex-managers[7] gave the new managers a document[8]. It read[9],

The managers of the Opera must pay the ghost 20,000 francs[10] a month — 240,000 francs a year.

Box 5 must also be available[11] for the ghost for every performance.

The two new managers laughed to themselves and forgot all about the ghost. They thought it was nonsense[1]. But a few days later they received a strange letter written in red. The writing[2] was very childlike[3]. It read,

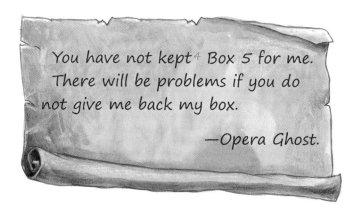

You have not kept[4] Box 5 for me. There will be problems if you do not give me back my box.

—Opera Ghost.

1. **nonsense** [ˋnɑːnsns] (n.) 無意義的話
2. **writing** [ˋraɪtɪŋ] (n.) 筆跡
3. **childlike** [ˋtʃaɪldlaɪk] (a.) 似小孩的
4. **keep** [kiːp] (v.) 保留
5. **serious** [ˋsɪrɪəs] (a.) 嚴重的;不幸的
6. **consequence** [ˋkɑːnsəkwens] (n.) 後果;結果
7. **former** [ˋfɔːrmə(r)] (a.) 以前的;在前的
8. **joke** [dʒouk] (v.) 開玩笑
9. **ignore** [ɪgˋnɔː(r)] (v.) 忽略

The next day, they received another letter written in the same red childlike writing.

It read,

You must pay me my
20,000 francs.
If you do not, there will
be serious[5] consequences[6].

—Opera Ghost.

The new managers said, "It is the former[7] managers. They think it's funny to joke[8] about this ghost. Let's just ignore[9] it."

Soon after, they sold Box 5.

One Point Lesson

● The next day, they received another letter **(which is)** written in the same red childlike writing.
第二天，他們收到另一封信，一樣也是紅色的字，筆跡像小孩。

若關係代名詞當「**受詞**」使用，則關係代名詞 **who**、**which**、**that** 可省略，但若是關係代名詞前面**有介係詞**或**逗號**時不可省略，也不可用 that 代換。

e.g. A girl **(who was)** named Mary lived here.
一個名叫瑪莉的女孩住在這裡。

The next few days passed by[1] without any problems in the theater. However, one evening, the owners of Box 5 started behaving[2] very strangely. During the performance, they were laughing and shouting.

Managers Moncharmin and Richard asked the guard[3], "What happened in Box 5 last night?" The guard said, "Well, the people in that box said that a voice told them, 'Box 5 is taken.' Then the people behaved terribly."

"What did the box-keeper say?" asked the managers.
"She said it was the ghost," replied the guard.

1. **pass by**（時間）過去
2. **behave** [bɪˋheɪv] (v.)
   行為舉止
3. **guard** [gɑːrd] (n.)
   警衛；守衛
4. **bring** [brɪŋ] (v.) 帶來
5. **demand** [dɪˋmand] (v.) 要求
6. **footstool** [ˋfʊtstuːl] (n.) 腳凳
7. **burst out** 突然……起來
8. **fire** [ˋfaɪə(r)] (v.)
   開除；解雇

"Bring[4] the box-keeper here now!" they demanded[5].

The box-keeper, Madame Giry, came.

"It was the ghost, sirs," she said. "He's very angry about the box and his money."

"Has he ever spoken to you?" the managers asked.

"Yes, of course. He asked me for a footstool[6]," she replied.

The managers burst out[7] laughing.

The woman was very serious, however.

The managers decided to fire[8] the box-keeper.

A Choose the synonym of the word underlined.

❶ The gala performance was a complete <u>triumph</u>.

(a) success (b) disaster

(c) intensity (d) superb

❷ He felt a sharp pain in his <u>chest</u>.

(a) brain   (b) heart

(c) shoulder (d) back

❸ The managers decided to <u>fire</u> the box-keeper.

(a) quit   (b) retire

(c) hire   (d) sack

B Fill in the blanks with the given words.
Remember to change the form of the verbs.

what happen	in private	outshine

❶ _____ _____ in Box 5 last night?

❷ I would like to speak to you _____ _____.

❸ But no performance _____ Christine Daae's.

C True or False.

T F ❶ Christine fainted during her performance.

T F ❷ When Raoul entered Christine's room, there was a man in the room.

T F ❸ In the dressing room, Christine denied remembering Raoul.

T F ❹ After Raoul left Christine's room, he heard her say, "I only sing for you, Raoul."

T F ❺ The two new managers received a strange letter written in red.

D Complete the sentences with the given words in past perfect tense.

❶ All of the dancers, composers and singers *(work)* _____ in perfect harmony.

❷ She *(never be)* _____ the best singer but tonight she was like a flower in full bloom.

❸ Raoul *(come)* _____ to the performance with his brother.

❹ Raoul *(grow)* _____ into a successful, well-balanced, young man.

Chapter Three

The Angel of Music

Christine did not appear in public[1] after the gala performance. She seemed to disappear completely. Raoul wrote letters to her, asking if he could come to see her. He received no reply[2], and then a letter from Christine came to his house.

1. **in public** 公開地
2. **reply** [rɪˋplaɪ] (n.)
   答覆；回答
3. **monsieur** [məsyör] (n.)
   先生；閣下（法語的敬稱，同英語中的 Sir 或 Mr.）
4. **anniversary** [͵ænɪˋvɜːrsəri] (n.) 週年紀念
5. **bury** [ˋberi] (v.) 埋葬；安葬

Monsieur[3],

I have not forgotten the little boy who went into the sea for my scarf. I feel I must write to you today as I am going to the country. Tomorrow is the anniversary[4] of the death of my father who liked you. He is buried[5] with his violin where we played when we were children.

Christine

Raoul decided to follow[6] Christine, to the inn[7] in the country where she was going.

During his long train journey[8] the next day, memories from his childhood[9] came back to him.

6. **follow** [ˋfɑːloʊ] (v.) 跟；隨
7. **inn** [ɪn] (n.) 旅館
8. **journey** [ˋdʒɜːrni] (n.) 旅程；旅行
9. **childhood** [ˋtʃaɪldhʊd] (n.) 幼年時期

When Raoul was a boy, he met Christine and her father, Mr. Daae. Raoul fell in love with[1] Christine when he heard her sing while her father played the violin in a small town.

It was a windy[2] day and the wind had carried[3] her scarf into the sea. Raoul went into the water and brought it back to her and they had been friends ever since[4].

They spent many happy days together and Christine's father told them many exciting[5] stories. One story he told was of the Angel of Music. He said a person could sing or play music well only if[6] he or she had seen the Angel of Music.

Many years had passed.
On the day Raoul saw Christine at the Opera, his old love for her returned.

1. **fall in love with** 愛上
2. **windy** [ˋwɪndi] (a.) 風強的
3. **carry** [ˋkæri] (v.) 傳送；運送
4. **ever since** 自從
5. **exciting** [ɪkˋsaɪtɪŋ] (a.) 令人興奮的
6. **only if** 只要；只有

When Raoul arrived at the small inn in the country, Christine was waiting for him.

"I'm so glad[1] you came," she said.

"I am so confused[2]. Why did you pretend[3] not to know me in your dressing room that night?" he asked.

She didn't reply.

Raoul said angrily, "Because there is another man. I heard his voice. He was in the room with you."

"What do you mean[4]?" she asked.

She seemed a little afraid.

"I heard you say, 'I only sing for you.'"

Then you said, "I gave you my soul tonight," Raoul said.

"What else[5] did you hear?" she cried.

"He said, 'You must love me.' Who is he, Christine?"

"Tell me everything you heard!" she insisted.

Raoul told her everything he had heard and done that night.

"It's the Angel of Music," Christine said. "That was the voice you heard. He has been giving me singing lessons for three months now."

Raoul did not believe in[6] the story of the Angel of Music but he was very confused.

1. **glad** [glæd] (a.) 高興的
2. **confused** [kənˋfjuːzd] (a.) 困惑的；不安的
3. **pretend** [prɪˋtend] (v.) 假裝
4. **mean** [miːn] (v.) 意指；意謂
5. **else** [els] (adv.) 其他；另外
6. **believe in** 相信；信任

Later that evening, Christine left the inn. Secretly, Raoul followed her in the darkness. She walked to her father's grave[1]. It was a very strange night. It was deathly silent, and there were clouds[2] of mist[3] throughout[4] the graveyard[5]. He could see Christine kneeling[6] beside her father's grave.

He heard some strange music coming from the sky. He was about to[7] walk closer when some skulls rolled[8] across the ground in front of him. He jumped back in fright[9]. As he jumped back, he bumped into[10] a figure behind him. It was wearing a long cloak[11]. It seemed like pure[12] evil. The figure showed its face—— it was a skull with yellow skin and piercing[13] eyes. Raoul fainted[14] and fell to the ground.

1. **grave** [greɪv] (n.)
   墳墓；墓地
2. **cloud** [klaud] (n.)
   一大群；一大片
3. **mist** [mɪst] (n.) 霧；靄
4. **throughout** [θruˋaut]
   (prep.) 遍及；遍布
5. **graveyard** [ˋgreɪvjɑːrd]
   (n.) 墓地
6. **kneel** [niːl] (v.) 跪下

7. **be about to** 即將
8. **roll** [roul] (v.) 滾動；移動
9. **fright** [fraɪt] (n.) 驚駭
10. **bump into** 無意間碰到
11. **cloak** [klouk] (n.) 斗蓬
12. **pure** [pjur] (a.) 純粹的
13. **piercing** [ˋpɪrsɪŋ] (a.)
    尖銳的；銳利的
14. **faint** [feɪnt] (v.) 昏倒

Meanwhile[1], back at the Opera House, the managers had examined[2] Box 5 but they had found nothing strange in it.

A few days later, however, they received another letter. There were four demands[3].

1. Give me Box 5.
2. Christine Daae must sing the role[4] of Margherita tonight.
3. My box-keeper must return to work.
4. Pay me 20,000 francs a month.
If you do not do these things, something terrible will happen in tonight's performance of Faust.

— Opera Ghost

1. **meanwhile** [`mi:nwaɪl] (adv.) 其間;同時
2. **examine** [ɪg`zæmɪn] (v.) 仔細檢查
3. **demand** [dɪ`mænd] (n.) 要求
4. **role** [roʊl] (n.) 角色
5. **be tired of** 對……厭煩

The managers were very angry.
They were tired of[5] the joke.

There were other problems as well[6].
That night, the head[7] groom[8] entered the
managers' office and said, "Someone stole[9]
one of the horses. I think it was the ghost.
I saw a dark figure riding[10] away in the
darkness."

6. **as well** 也；同樣地
7. **head** [hed] (a.) 等級最高的
8. **groom** [gru:m] (n.) 馬伕
9. **steal** [sti:l] (v.) 偷竊
   (steal-stole-stolen)
10. **ride** [raɪd] (v.) 騎馬
    (ride-rode-ridden)

Also that night, Carlotta, one of the most important singers in the Opera House, sat in her dressing room reading a letter. It read,

Dear Carlotta,

Do not sing in tonight's performance of Faust.

If you do, a tragedy[1] worse than death will befall[2] you.

Carlotta thought deeply about the letter. She was nervous[3], but if she did not sing tonight, Christine would. She was jealous[4] of Christine, so she decided to sing.

1. **tragedy** [ˋtradʒədi] (n.) 悲劇
2. **befall** [bɪˋfɔːl] (v.)
   降臨；發生
3. **nervous** [ˋnɜːrvəs] (a.)
   緊張的；失措的
4. **jealous** [ˋdʒeləs] (a.)
   妒忌的

5. **full house** 客滿
6. **croak** [kroʊk] (n.)
   低沈粗嘎的聲音
7. **frog** [frɑːg] (n.) 青蛙
8. **chandelier** [ˌʃandəˋlɪr] (n.)
   大吊燈
9. **crash** [kræʃ] (v.) 撞擊

That night, it was a full house[5] for the performance of *Faust*. Carlotta started to sing. Soon she forgot all about the letter. Then something terrible happened. In the middle of a song, her voice went, "Croak[6]!" She sounded like a frog[7]. Everything became silent.

Just behind the managers, came a voice saying, "Her singing will make the chandelier fall."

Terrified, they looked up at the chandelier[8].

It fell and crashed[9] into the audience killing a woman.

A Match.

1 A stage-shifter •   • A A person who looks after horses.

2 A box-keeper •   • B A person who moves the stage scenery at a theater.

3 A groom •   • C A person who comes to the performances.

4 A manager •   • D A person who conducts the whole business.

5 An audience •   • E A person who takes the audience to their seat in the theater.

B Choose the correct answer.

1 How did Christine's singing improve?

(a) She was practicing alone in her room.

(b) The Angel of Music gave her singing lessons.

(c) Sorelli was teaching her.

2 Why did the new managers of the Opera ignore the letter?

(a) They didn't want to pay the 20,000 francs.

(b) They wanted to show the ghost that they were not scared.

(c) They thought that it was all a joke.

3 Why did Carlotta decide to sing in the performance?

(a) Because she was jealous of Christine and she did not want her to sing.

(b) Because she loved singing so much.

(c) Because she did not believe anything bad would happen.

C Fill in the blanks with the given words.

> deathly inn grave darkness kneeling mist

Late that evening, Christine left the **1**_____.
Secretly, Raoul followed her in the **2**_____. She
walked to her father's **3**_____. It was a very strange
night. It was **4**_____ silent and there were clouds
of **5**_____ throughout the graveyard. He could see
Christine **6**_____ beside her father's grave. He
heard some strange music coming from the sky.

Film and Stage Versions
of the Novel

When it was first published, no one thought Leroux's *The Phantom of the Opera* was a great novel that would be famous for a long time.

Many critics pointed out serious flaws in the story and called it a ghost story that was inferior to other similar stories. However, Leroux's idea of a ghost story set in a huge, mysterious opera house was a great idea for movies and plays.

The first of these films came out in 1927, and starred Lon Chaney. Several of Leroux's books had already been made into movies, but this film was the most successful.

More remakes were made throughout the following decades, along with several stage performances. The most famous stage production is Andrew Lloyd Webber's 1988 version. Webber returned to Leroux's original version of the story, but he removed the major flaws in the story. His efforts led to a world-famous stage musical that has been performed more than 7,000 times in several countries.

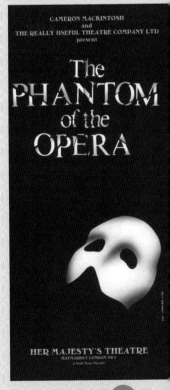

Chapter Four

The Man Beneath[1] the Opera House

After the disaster[2], Christine disappeared once again. Raoul tried to find her but he was unsuccessful. One evening, as he was walking home, he saw Christine in a carriage[3].

"Christine! Christine!" he shouted out. Then, he heard a man's voice. "Move on!" the voice said and the carriage moved away.

Raoul thought, "Christine really is in love with another man." The next morning, Raoul received a letter.

1. **beneath** [bɪ`ni:θ] (prep.) 在……下
2. **disaster** [dɪ`zæstə(r)] (n.) 災難
3. **carriage** [`kærɪdʒ] (n.) 四輪馬車

4. **a masked ball** 化妝舞會
5. **the day after tomorrow** 後天
6. **domino** [`dɑːmənoʊ] (n.) 化妝舞會中所穿的寬長袍

Dear Raoul,

There will be a masked ball[4] at the Opera House the day after tomorrow[5].

Come and wear a white domino[6].

I will meet you at midnight[7].

Christine

Raoul was filled with[8] hope. He read the letter excitedly and decided to go. But he thought, "Who is this Angel of Music? Is Christine in love with him or is she his prisoner[9]?"

His uncertainty[10] made him very nervous.

7. **midnight** [ˈmɪdnaɪt] (n.) 午夜

8. **be filled with** 充滿

9. **prisoner** [ˈprɪzənə(r)] (n.) 犯人；囚犯

10. **uncertainty** [ʌnˈsɜːrtnti] (n.) 不確定

The masked ball at the Opera was a big event. All of the richest and most famous people in Paris were there. Raoul went to the ball. It was almost midnight when someone wearing a black mask came to him. It was Christine.

She signaled[1] him to follow her.

They walked through crowds[2] of people, and he saw a large man in red wearing a large hat and a skull for a mask. Many people had gathered around him. Raoul could see some words on his cloak[3]. They said, "Do not touch me! I am Red Death!"

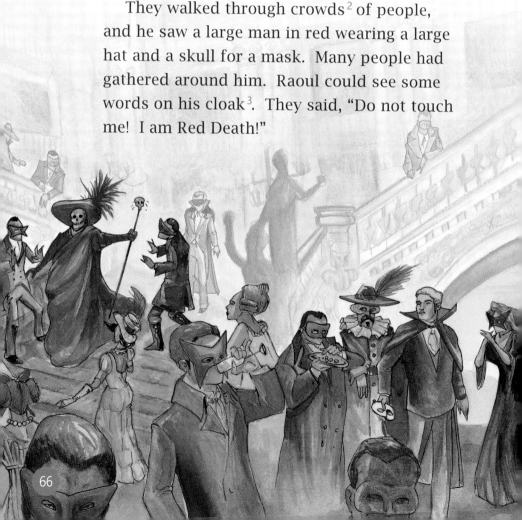

Raoul followed her into one of the Opera boxes. She said, "Don't worry. He doesn't know we are here."

But Raoul could see out into the corridor.

Red Death was coming down the corridor!

"He's coming. He's coming down the corridor," Raoul said.

"Who?" asked Christine.

"Red Death! Your Angel of Music! I want to see him. I want to take off[4] his mask," he replied.

"Please! No, don't do it," Christine cried out, blocking[5] his way.

"If you love me, please don't do it."

Raoul was very angry now.

"You love him, don't you?" he cried.

"Go! I won't stop you. But I hate you, Christine. You are treating[6] me so badly.

One moment you seem to love me, and the next moment it seems you don't. Go!"

Christine looked so sad.

1. **signal** [ˈsɪgnəl] (v.)
   打信號；示意
2. **crowd** [kraʊd] (n.)
   一堆；許多
3. **cloak** [kloʊk] (n.) 披風
4. **take off** 脫下
5. **block** [blɑːk] (v.)
   阻擋；妨礙
6. **treat** [triːt] (v.) 對待

23

"One day you will understand," she whispered[1]. "I have to go. Please don't follow me." Then, she left Raoul and went down the corridor.

The ball was still continuing, but Raoul did not want to return to it. He was not in the mood[2] to be drinking and dancing. Instead, he walked around the Opera House.

As he walked miserably[3], he found himself[4] walking toward Christine's dressing room.
He pushed the door open and went in.
A few seconds later, Christine came in.
She took off her black gloves and Raoul could see a gold ring on her hand.

"A wedding ring[5]," he wondered[6]. "Who gave it to her? Red Death?"

She sat down on a chair, put her head in her hands and sighed[7]. "Poor Erik! Poor Erik!"

1. **whisper** [ˈwɪspə(r)] (v.)
   低語
2. **mood** [muːd] (n.)
   心情；情緒
3. **miserably** [ˈmɪzərəbli] (adv.)
   可憐兮兮地
4. **find oneself**
   發現自己處於某種狀態
5. **wedding ring** 結婚戒指
6. **wonder** [ˈwʌndə(r)] (v.)
   感到疑惑；納悶

"Erik?" Raoul thought. "Who's Erik?"

Suddenly, Raoul heard a distant[8] sound of singing.

As he listened more closely, he realized the voice was coming closer and closer. Soon, it seemed as if the voice were in the room.

"Erik!" she cried out.

"You're late!" The voice still continued singing. It was singing "The Wedding-Night Song" from *Romeo and Juliet* and it was the most beautiful singing.

7. sigh [saɪ] (v.) 嘆息

8. distant [ˋdɪstənt] (a.)
來自遠方的；遙遠的

69

24

Raoul began to understand how Christine improved[1] so much. Christine stood up and walked toward a mirror. Raoul followed her, but he suddenly felt cold wind and the room began to spin[2] around. He didn't know what was happening. When everything finally stood still[3] again, Christine had disappeared from the room!

Raoul did not see Christine again until he went back to the Opera.

She seemed very happy to see him.

"Raoul, I'm so glad to see you!" she exclaimed[4]. "When do you leave for[5] the navy?"

"In a month's time," Raoul replied.

Christine suddenly looked very sad.

"Then we will part[6] forever in a month's time," she said very sadly.

---

1. **improve** [ɪm`pruːv] (v.)
   改善;增進
2. **spin** [spɪn] (v.) 旋轉
3. **stand still** 站著不動

4. **exclaim** [ɪk`skleɪm] (v.)
   大喊;驚叫
5. **leave for** 動身前往
6. **part** [pɑːrt] (v.) 分離;分開

"But we could be true[7] to each other. We can promise to be loyal[8] to each other," Raoul said.

With tears in her eyes, she replied, "I can never marry you Raoul." Then her sad expression[9] suddenly changed. "But we could be engaged[10] for a month. It would be our secret."

"Alright," agreed Raoul.
"Let's be engaged for a month."

7. **true** [tru:] (a.) 忠實的
8. **loyal** [ˋlɔɪəl] (a.)
   忠貞的；堅實的
9. **expression** [ɪkˋsprɛʃn] (n.)
   臉色；表情
10. **engaged** [ɪnˋgeɪdʒd] (a.)
   訂婚的

After making their promise[1] to each other, they spent[2] many happy days together at the Opera House. The building was very exciting, and Christine showed[3] Raoul all of it.

One day, they walked by an open trap door[4] and Raoul said, "You've shown me this whole building but not the underground[5] passageways[6]. Let's go down."
Christine's face turned white.
She looked terrified.

1. **make a promise** 許下承諾
2. **spend** [spend] (v.)
   花費；度過
3. **show** [ʃou] (v.) 展示；表現
4. **trap door** 活門
5. **underground**
   [ˋʌndɚˏɡraʊnd] (a.)
   地下的；秘密的

"No. We are not going down there.
That is his place," she said.
"Oh, so Erik lives down there, does he?" he
asked.

Christine walked away and said, "I don't
want to talk about it. We only have a short
time together. Let's enjoy it."
Raoul looked back at the trap door. It was
now shut. "He shut[7] it, didn't he?" he asked.

Christine didn't answer. She just walked
away. Raoul ran after her and said, "Look, if
you are afraid of him, I can help you. I can
take you away where he can never find you."
She looked at Raoul with great hope[8].

---

6. **passageway** [`pæsɪdʒweɪ]
   (n.) 通道；走廊
   (= corridor)

7. **shut** [ʃʌt] (v.) 關閉
   (shut-shut-shut)

8. **with great hope** 充滿希望

26

Christine took Raoul's hand and led[1] him up to the roof[2] of the Opera House.

"We can talk safely here," she said. "I'll tell you everything. Raoul, you know that I never had a really good voice. Well, one night, I heard the most beautiful voice through the walls. I asked if he was the Angel of Music and he said that he was. We became great friends, and he taught me how to improve my voice. My singing became wonderful because of him. Then, one day I saw you in the audience, and I fell in love with you again. I told the Angel of Music about you and he became very jealous[3]. He said I had to choose between you and him. I was so afraid of losing[4] him, so I pretended that I didn't know you that day in my dressing room."

"I see," said Raoul.

1. **lead** [li:d] (v.) 帶路；引導
   (lead-led-led)
2. **roof** [ru:f] (n.) 屋頂
3. **jealous** [ˋdʒeləs] (a.)
   嫉妒的
4. **lose** [lu:z] (v.) 失去
   (lose-lost-lost)
5. **continue** [kənˋtɪnjuː] (v.)
   繼續

Christine continued[5]. "That night when the chandelier fell, I was very afraid, and I went to my dressing room. But everything was different. I walked toward the mirror but then it moved and I found myself in a very strange place."

Raoul thought, "Yes. That's like when I was hiding there."

27

"Everything was so dark. Then I saw something come toward me. It picked me up[1] and put me on a horse. We rode off[2] together down through the Opera House cellars until we came to an underground lake. He put me into a boat and took me to a house in the middle of this lake.

1. **pick up** 舉起

2. **ride off** 乘馬離開
   (ride-rode-ridden)

In the house, I could see him more clearly but . . . he wore a very dark strange mask.

He put me on a sofa and said, 'Do not be afraid.' He spoke very gently[3] to me. 'I am not the Angel of Music. I am Erik. I am just a man, not a ghost,' he said. 'Please stay here with me for five days. I am in love with you. I will let you go[4] after five days. I promise to let you go as long as[5] you never see my face.'

Then I did a stupid thing. I grabbed[6] his mask away and saw his face. It was just like a skull with piercing eyes.

He shouted at me, 'You will never leave this house now that you have seen my face. You would never come back to see me again. So I will never let you leave.' Then he left me alone for a while."

3. **gently** [`dʒentli] (adv.)
   溫柔地;溫和地
4. **let A go** 讓 A 離開
5. **as long as** 只要

6. **grab** [græb] (v.)
   攫取;抓住
   (grab-grabbed-grabbed)

🎧 28

"What happened after that?" Raoul asked.

"Well, I decided to show him I wasn't afraid of his face. I really wanted to leave that house. Even though[1] he frightened[2] me so much, I knew that it was the only way[3].

At last, he let me go."

"Did you go back?" asked Raoul.

"Yes," she answered.

"Why?" the young man asked.

"Because I feel sorry for him. He is very lonely. Everyone who sees his face is afraid of him," she replied.

1. **even though** 雖然；即使
2. **frighten** [ˋfraɪtn] (v.)
   使驚恐；使害怕
3. **the only way** 唯一的方法
4. **in terror** 恐懼地

Just then they looked up to see
the horrible figure coming toward
them. Christine took Raoul's hand,
and they ran to the other end of the roof and
down the stairs in terror[4].

A Choose the correct answer.

1 Christine really is _____ love with another man.

    (a) on   (b) to   (c) in   (d) of

2 I want to take _____ his mask and see his face.

    (a) on   (b) with   (c) of   (d) off

3 Raoul read Christine's letter and he was filled _____ hope.

    (a) with   (b) of   (c) by   (d) on

B Choose the word irrelevant to the other words of the category.

1 (a) cellar   (b) ball

    (c) corridor   (d) roof

2 (a) phantom   (b) dancers

    (c) scene-shifters   (d) chorus-master

3 (a) frightened   (b) scared

    (c) terrified   (d) exhausted

C Rearrange the sentences in chronological order.

1 Raoul went to the masked ball.

2 Raoul and Christine promised to be engaged for a month.

3 Raoul received a letter from Christine.

4 Raoul found that Christine had disappeared in her room.

_____ ⇨ _____ ⇨ _____ ⇨ _____

D Fill in the blanks with the given words.

until   as   even though   because   when

1 I really wanted to leave that house and _____ he frightened me so much, I knew it was the only way.

2 We rode off together down through the Opera cellars _____ we came to a lake.

3 _____ he listened more closely, he realized the voice was coming closer and closer.

4 It was almost midnight _____ someone wearing a black mask came to him.

5 He wouldn't let me leave the house _____ I had seen his face.

Chapter Five

🎧29 Christine Disappears

Christine and Raoul ran through the Opera House to get away from[1] Erik.

Suddenly a man stepped[2] into their way[3]. He had very dark skin[4] and wore clothing from a middle-eastern[5] country.

"Go down there," he said. They went in the direction[6] that the man had pointed[7]. They finally came to Christine's room.

1. **get away from** 從……離開
2. **step** [step] (v.) 踏；踩
3. **way** [weɪ] (n.) 通道；路
4. **skin** [skɪn] (n.) 皮膚
5. **middle-eastern** 中東的
6. **direction** [dəˋrekʃn] (n.) 方向；方位
7. **point** [pɔɪnt] (v.) 指

"Who was that man?" Raoul asked.

"That's the Persian. He's always here at the Opera House," she replied.

"Christine! I want you to come away with me now. It's ridiculous[8] to have to live like this," said Raoul.

"Not today," she replied. "I promised I would sing at tomorrow's performance for Erik.

I must do that. I will go away with you after the performance."

They discussed[9] their plans to run away[10] the next evening.

8. **ridiculous** [rɪ`dɪkjələs] (a.) 荒謬的；可笑的
9. **discuss** [dɪ`skʌs] (v.) 討論
10. **run away** 逃跑 (= get away)

30

The next day, Raoul prepared for the evening. He ordered a carriage to be ready outside the Opera at the end of the performance.

The Opera House was crowded[1] that night. Everyone had come to listen to Christine. She sang nervously[2] at first[3], but she finally relaxed and gave her best performance ever. The audience went wild and gave her a standing ovation[4]. Suddenly, all the lights went out[5]. Everything was in complete darkness. Then there was a scream[6] — it was a woman's voice.

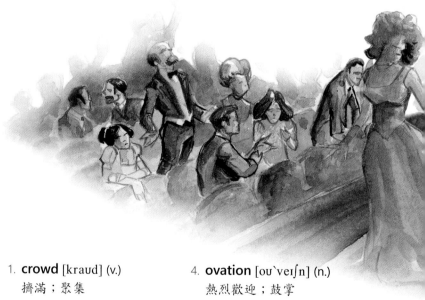

1. **crowd** [kraʊd] (v.)
   擠滿；聚集
2. **nervously** [ˋnɜːrvəsli] (adv.)
   緊張地
3. **at first** 起初；一開始

4. **ovation** [oʊˋveɪʃn] (n.)
   熱烈歡迎；鼓掌
5. **go out** 熄滅
6. **scream** [skriːm] (n.) 尖叫
7. **turn on** 點亮

The managers quickly had the lights turned on[7] again, but Christine had disappeared.

There was a loud murmuring[8] of voices in the audience. Raoul was very worried.

He hurried[9] to the managers' office to find out what was going on.

As he was about to enter the office, he felt a hand on his shoulder. It was the Persian man.

"Don't talk about Erik with anyone," he warned[10]. Then, he put his finger to his lips, signaling secrecy[11].

8. **murmuring** [ˈmɝːmə(r)ɪŋ]
   (n.) 低語；低聲抱怨
9. **hurry** [ˈhɝːri] (v.)
   趕緊去；匆忙
10. **warn** [wɔːrn] (v.)
    告誡；提醒
11. **secrecy** [ˈsiːkrəsi]
    (n.) 秘密

31

Raoul went into the managers' office. There were many men there including[1] a detective[2]. They all looked at Raoul suspiciously[3]. The detective asked him, "You've been spending a lot of time with Miss Daae, haven't you?"

1. **including** [ɪn`kluːdɪŋ]
   (prep.) 包括；包含
2. **detective** [dɪ`tektɪv] (n.)
   偵探
3. **suspiciously** [sə`spɪʃəsli]
   (adv.) 疑惑地；猜疑地
4. **friendship** [`frendʃɪp] (n.)
   友誼；友情

5. **That's none of your business.** 不關你的事
6. **furious** [`fjurɪəs] (a.)
   盛怒的
7. **Count** [kaunt] (n.) 伯爵

"Yes," replied Raoul.

"You were going to leave with Miss Daae after the performance tonight, weren't you?"

"Yes, that's true."

"Your brother wasn't happy about your friendship[4] with Miss Daae, was he?"

"That's none of your business[5]," Raoul replied angrily.

"Did you know that your brother's carriage was outside the Opera House tonight but now it's gone?" the detective asked Raoul. "Your brother took Miss Daae!"

Raoul was furious[6] now.

"I'll find them," he shouted.

After Raoul left the room, the detective, smiling, said, "I don't know if the Count[7] took Miss Daae but Raoul will find out for us!"

One Point Lesson

◆ Your brother **wasn't** happy about your friendship with Miss Daae, **was he?**
你哥哥不太高興你和戴伊小姐來往，是吧？

附加問句：簡短的 yes-no 問句，附加於直述句之後，往往用來取得對方的同意，或是驗證剛剛所說的話，未必期待對方的回答。

e.g. You **were** going to leave with Miss Daae after the performance tonight, **weren't you?** 今晚表演結束後，你就會和戴伊小姐一起離開，不是嗎？

32

When Raoul rushed[1] out of the office,
the Persian blocked[2] his way.
"Where are you going?" he asked Raoul.
"I'm going to find Christine Daae,"
Raoul replied.
"Then start looking in the Opera House.
She left through the cellars."

Raoul, surprised, said, "How do you know?"
"Erik has taken her through a secret
passage to the house on the lake," the Persian
man said quietly.

"You seem to know so much about Erik.
What else do you know?" Raoul asked.
"He's extremely[3] dangerous."
"Did he hurt[4] you?" asked the young man.
The Persian replied, "I have forgiven him
for all that."

1. **rush** [rʌʃ] (v.) 衝;奔
2. **block** [blɑːk] (v.) 阻擋
3. **extremely** [ɪk`striːmli] (adv.) 極其;非常
4. **hurt** [hɜːrt] (v.) 傷害;使受傷
5. **monster** [`mɑːnstə(r)] (n.) 怪物;邪惡的人

"You are the same as Christine," said Raoul. "You both think he is a monster[5] but you both feel sorry for him."

"Shhh," hushed[6] the Persian.

"He may hear us. He could be anywhere — the floor, the walls, the ceiling."

The two men went to Christine's room. The Persian went to the mirror and knocked on[7] the wall.

Suddenly the mirror began to revolve[8].

"Hurry," he said to Raoul. "We are going to the cellars[9]. Be careful and do exactly[10] what I tell you."

6. **hush** [hʌʃ] (v.) 使安靜
7. **knock on** 敲；擊
8. **revolve** [rɪˋvɑːlv] (v.) 旋轉

9. **cellar** [ˋselə(r)] (n.) 地下室；地窖
10. **exactly** [ɪgˋzæktli] (adv.) 確切地；精確地

🎧 33

They walked through the dark cellars.

Raoul could hear mice and rats[1] running along the damp[2] floors.

They walked until they came to a wall.

1. **rat** [ræt] (n.) 鼠
2. **damp** [dæmp] (a.) 潮濕的
3. **entrance** [`entrəns] (n.) 入口
4. **direct** [də`rekt] (v.) 引導；對準
5. **lever** [`levər] (n.) 控制桿
6. **pull** [pʊl] (v.) 拉

"This is an entrance[3] to Erik's house.

Buquet died here. He discovered the house and Erik killed him to keep it a secret."

He directed[4] his lamp on the wall.

"There's a lever[5] here. We pull[6] it, and the door opens. Here it is!"

The wall opened and they walked in.

Soon the wall slammed[7] shut behind them. They were in an empty room.

The walls were made of[8] glass.

"The walls are mirrors!" exclaimed Raoul.

"It's Erik's torture[9] chamber[10].

We have to find a way out[11] quickly,"

said the Persian in a desperate[12] voice.

7. **slam** [slæm] (v.) 猛地關上
8. **be made of** 由……製造
9. **torture** [`tɔːrtʃə(r)] (n.)
   酷刑;折磨
10. **chamber** [`tʃeɪmbə(r)] (n.)
   房間;室
11. **way out** 出口;出路
12. **desperate** [`despərət] (a.)
   絕望的

A Fill in the blanks with the given words.

didn't he	isn't she	did they
will they	have you	wasn't she

1 He shut it, _____?

2 They didn't like the food, _____?

3 She was going to marry him, _____?

4 You haven't been to the Opera yet, _____?

5 They won't mind if we borrow the book, _____?

6 She is going to sing in the performance tonight, _____?

B Rearrange the sentences in chronological order.

1 Raoul met the Persian outside of the managers' office.

2 Christine suddenly disappeared during her performance.

3 They walked through dark cellars filled with rats and mice.

4 They walked into Erik's room of mirrors.

5 A detective questioned Raoul very suspiciously.

6 The Persian opened the secret door in Christine's room.

_____ ⇨ _____ ⇨ _____ ⇨ _____ ⇨ _____ ⇨ _____

C Match.

1. If you pull this lever,   • • **A** if you want to borrow it.

2. I will meet you tomorrow • • **B** you will be late

3. I will lend you my book   • • **C** if you want to come with me.

4. I will go to the movies   • • **D** the door will open.

5. If you don't leave now,   • • **E** if you call me to tell me what time to meet.

D True or False.

T F 1. Raoul wanted to take Christine away to a safe place.

T F 2. Raoul knew his brother took Christine.

T F 3. The detective wanted Raoul to help find Christine.

T F 4. The Persian knew who took Christine.

T F 5. The Persian did not feel sorry for Erik.

People
in the Opera House

In the time of Leroux's novel, the Paris Opera House employed more than 1,500 people. Although the public did not see most of these people, they were needed.

Ticket sellers, ushers and box-keepers helped the audience members with their seats. To change scenes on the stage, up to 110 carpenters were needed. Then stagehands, gasmen and firemen would follow to lay carpet, light lamps and make sure no fires would start. More than one hundred extras were used to represent people in the background of the scenes. These people played soldiers, townspeople, and the like. Almost one hundred ballet dancers, and about 120 opera singers would perform on the stage.

Painters were employed to keep the props looking beautiful and make up artists kept the performers looking their best. The managers of the Opera even hired people to clap at certain points of the performance! It took an amazing amount of effort and teamwork to put on a performance.

Chapter Six

In the House on the Lake

🎧 34

While[1] they tried to find a way out of Erik's torture chamber, the Persian told Raoul about Erik's history. He'd had a difficult life.

1. **while** [waɪl] (conj.)
   當……的時候
2. **Persia** [pɝːrʃə] (n.) 波斯

3. **Sultan** [`sʌltən] (n.)
   蘇丹王；伊斯蘭教國王
4. **talented** [`tæləntɪd] (a.)
   有天賦的

"We have a very long history together," he explained. "We both worked in Persia[2] many years ago. I was a policeman and Erik worked for the Sultan[3]. Erik was a very intelligent and talented[4] architect[5]. He designed magical[6] buildings with secret passages for the Sultan to hide[7] in when he feared for his life.

The Sultan also commanded[8] Erik to build torture chambers for him.
He was fascinated[9] by Erik's clever creativity[10].
Erik was not only a creative[11] architect, but he was a powerful and passionate[12] singer. He still is," continued the Persian.

5. **architect** [ˋɑrkɪtekt] (n.) 建築師
6. **magical** [ˋmædʒɪkl] (a.) 神秘的；有魔力的
7. **hide** [haɪd] (v.) 躲藏
8. **command** [kəˋmænd] (v.) 命令
9. **fascinate** [ˋfæsɪneɪt] (v.) 吸引；使著迷
10. **creativity** [ˌkriːeɪˋtɪvəti] (n.) 創造力
11. **creative** [kriˋeɪtɪv] (a.) 有創造力的
12. **passionate** [ˋpæʃənət] (a.) 熱情的

35

"I really hated the work Erik did but respected him for his intelligence and his wonderful singing ability. Erik has done some evil things in his life, but I have always felt sorry for him. People have laughed at[1] him and rejected[2] him all his life because he is so ugly.

In the end, the Sultan in Persia tried to have him killed. He didn't want him working for anyone else. I helped him to escape, and he eventually found his way to France.

1. **laugh at** 嘲笑
2. **reject** [rɪ`dʒɛkt] (v.) 拒絕
3. **as well as** 也；和
4. **closely** [klousli] (adv.) 仔細地
5. **involve** [ɪn`vɑːlv] (v.) 涉及；捲入
6. **trap** [træp] (v.) 落入陷阱

In France, Erik designed this Opera House. After years of designing secret passages and doors for the Sultan, it was very easy for him to build secret passages in this building as well as[3] a secret house on the lake. I always watched Erik very closely[4]. I was very worried when Christine became involved[5] with him."

Raoul listened carefully to the Persian's story. They were still trapped[6] in the room of mirrors.

36

Suddenly, they heard Erik's voice on the other side of the wall.

"Decide!" he shouted. "The wedding-mass[1] or the requiem[2]-mass. The choice is yours, Christine."

Christine gave a cry of pain.

Raoul looked desperate. He wanted to save[3] her from the monster. Then, they heard a gentle voice.

"Please do not be afraid of me. I am not an evil man. I just need you to love me, Christine."

1. **mass** [mæs] (n.) 彌撒（曲）
2. **requiem** [`rekwiem] (n.) 安魂曲；輓歌
3. **save** [seɪv] (v.) 拯救
4. **in the distance** 在遠處
5. **bell** [bel] (n.) 鐘聲；鈴聲
6. **dare** [der] (v.) 膽敢；勇於
7. **roar** [rɔ:(r)] (v.) 咆哮
8. **footstep** [`fʊtstep] (n.) 腳步聲

There was no reply from her. In the distance[4], there was the sound of a bell[5].

"Who dares[6] to come near my house?" roared[7] Erik. "I will be back, Christine."

Raoul and the Persian heard Erik's footsteps[8] leaving the room.

37

"If we call out to Christine, maybe she can come and free[1] us," Raoul said. "Christine! Christine!" he called out softly[2]. Christine heard him.

"Raoul! Where are you?" she called back.

"We're trapped in the room next to you. Can you let us out[3]?" he asked.

"I can't move. Erik has tied me up[4]. He said he would kill everyone if I won't marry him. He said he would kill himself too. He's gone mad," she cried out.

Raoul and the Persian knew they were in a dangerous situation. They desperately[5] searched for[6] a lever to open a trapdoor in the floor of the room. The Persian finally found it.

1. **free** [friː] (v.) 釋放
2. **softly** [ˋsɔːftli] (adv.) 輕聲地
3. **let A out** 讓 A 出來
4. **tie up** 繫牢;綁緊
5. **desperately** [ˋdespərətli] (adv.) 拼命地;絕望地
6. **search for** 搜尋
7. **wine cellar** 酒窖
8. **barrel** [ˋbærəl] (n.) 木桶
9. **gunpowder** 火藥
10. **blow up** 爆炸

The door opened and they ran down into a cellar.

"It's a wine cellar[7]," said Raoul.

There were a lot of barrels[8] in the cellar.

"Yes, but I don't think there is wine in these barrels," said the Persian. He opened one of the barrels and inside, there was gunpowder[9].

"He's going to blow up[10] the Opera House if Christine doesn't marry him," he cried.

38

They ran back to the torture chamber and cried out, "Christine!"

"I'm still here. He came back and said the visitor was dead. I . . . I . . . think he killed him," she told them in a frightened voice.

"Christine! Erik is going to blow up the Opera House if you don't marry him," Raoul warned[1] her. Just then, Erik returned.

"Who were you talking to?" he asked Christine. Then, he looked at the wall of the torture chamber. He crossed[2] the room and knocked on the wall.

1. **warn** [wɔːrn] (v.)
   警告；叮嚀
2. **cross** [krɔːs] (v.)
   穿過；越過
3. **shape** [ʃeɪp] (n.) 形狀

4. **grasshopper**
   [ˋɡræshɑːpə(r)] (n.) 蚱蜢
5. **scorpion** [ˋskɔːrpiən] (n.) 蠍
6. **refuse** [rɪˋfjuːz] (v.) 拒絕

"So Raoul has arrived, has he?" he said with an evil laugh.

Christine begged him, "Please let him go!"

"Then you must decide what you are going to do," he demanded.

"There are two boxes on the table. One is in the shape[3] of a grasshopper[4] and the other in the shape of a scorpion[5].

You must turn one of them. If you turn the scorpion, you agree to marry me. If you turn the grasshopper, then you refuse[6]. You must decide now, Christine," he said.

Then, he walked out of the room.

🎧 39

"If she turns the grasshopper, the gunpowder in the cellar will explode[1]," said the Persian.

They could hear her crying in the next room.

"What should I do? What should I do?" she cried out. Erik returned.

"Well, what will it be?" he asked her.

She turned the box with the scorpion on it. Beneath[2] them, the Persian and Raoul heard water flowing[3].

"He's flooding[4] the cellar," said the Persian.

The water filled the cellar and then began coming up through the trap door!

Soon, the chamber was full of water, and they were fighting for their lives. They both lost consciousness[5] soon after.

1. **explode** [ɪk`sploʊd] (v.) 爆炸
2. **beneath** [bɪ`niːθ] (prep.) 在⋯⋯下
3. **flow** [floʊ] (v.)（水）流
4. **flood** [flʌd] (v.) 淹沒；氾濫
5. **lose consciousness** 失去意識
6. **wake** [weɪk] (v.) 醒來
7. **fall asleep** 沈睡

The Persian woke[6] to find himself lying on a sofa. Erik was standing beside him. Christine was there too.

"You are alright now. Christine begged me to let you live. I did it for her," Erik told the Persian.

He gave the Persian something to drink, and the Persian soon fell asleep[7].

A few days passed[1].

The Persian was sitting on a sofa in his apartment. He had read all the stories about the events at the Opera House. Raoul's brother had been found dead near the underground lake. The newspapers also reported[2] the disappearance[3] of Raoul and Christine.

Persian's servant[4] came into the room, followed by a visitor. It was Erik.

"You are a murderer[5]!" the Persian accused[6] Erik. "Why did you kill Raoul's brother?"

Erik replied, "I didn't kill him. He must have drowned[7] in the lake. I came here to tell you that this is the last time you will see me. I am dying."

The Persian was filled with sympathy[8] for the sad, lonely man.

---

1. **pass** [pæs] (v.) 經過
2. **report** [rɪ`pɔːrt] (v.) 報導
3. **disappearance**
   [͵dɪsə`pɪrəns] (n.)
   消失；不見
4. **servant** [`sɜːrvənt] (n.) 僕人
5. **murderer** [`mɜːrdərə(r)] (n.)
   殺人兇手
6. **accuse** [ə`kjuːz] (v.) 指控
7. **drown** [draʊn] (v.) 溺死
8. **sympathy** [`sɪmpəθi] (n.)
   同情；憐憫

"I am ready to die now. She allowed[9] me to kiss her before I rescued[10] you and Raoul. Even my own mother never kissed me. When I kissed Christine, it was like all the angels in heaven were singing," Erik continued.

"Where are they now?" asked the Persian man. "They are safe. I gave them a wedding ring, and told them to be happy together," said Erik.

The Persian could see the tears in Erik's eyes. Erik left and the Phantom of the Opera disappeared forever.

9. **allow** [ə`lau] (v.)
   允許；准許
10. **rescue** [`reskju:] (v.)
   救助；援救

A Read the four sentences and write down who said each one.

Raoul   Erik   Christine   The Persian

1 We're trapped in the room next to you. _____

2 He said he would kill himself too. _____

3 I rescued you and Raoul for Christine. _____

4 I don't think there is wine in these barrels. _____

B Match.

1 fascinated • • **A** To be foolish or laughable.

2 creative • • **B** To do something with intense feeling.

3 sympathy • • **C** To be very interested by something.

4 passionate • • **D** To be able to invent and think of a new one.

5 ridiculous • • **E** To feel sad and pity on another's pain.

C Choose the correct answer.

❶ Why did the Sultan of Persia want to kill Erik?

(a) Because Erik knew too many of his secrets.

(b) Because he did a bad job designing the buildings.

(c) Because he didn't want him to work for anyone else.

❷ What did Erik threaten to do if Christine didn't marry him?

(a) He threatened to kill everyone and himself.

(b) He threatened to kill Raoul.

(c) He threatened to kill Christine.

D Make sentences with given words and "because of."

> **Rain   could not go   picnic**
> ⇨ Because of the rain, I could not go on the picnic.

❶ My homework   could not go   the movie

⇨ _____

❷ Heavy traffic   was late   school

⇨ _____

❸ Him   she improved her singing ability

⇨ _____

Appendixes

1 Basic Grammar

要增強英文閱讀理解能力，應練習找出英文的主結構。
要擁有良好的英語閱讀能力，首先要理解英文的段落結構。

「英文的閱讀理解從「分解文章」開始」

英文的文章是以「有意義的詞組」（指帶有意義的語句）
所構成的。用（／）符號來區別各個意義語塊，請試著掌握其
中的意義。

He knew / that she told a lie / at the party.

他知道　　　　她說了謊　　　　在舞會上

⇨ 他知道她在舞會上說謊的事。

As she was walking / in the garden, / she smelled /

當她行走　　　　在花園　　　她聞到味道

something wet.

某樣東西濕濕的

⇨ 她走在花園時聞到潮溼的味道。

一篇文章，要分成幾個有意義的詞組？

可放入（／）符號來區隔有意義詞組的地方，一般是在（1）「主詞＋動詞」之後；（2）and 和 but 等連接詞之前；（3）that、who 等關係代名詞之前；（4）副詞子句的前後，會用（／）符號來區隔。初學者可能在一篇文章中畫很多（／）符號，但隨著閱讀實力的提升，（／）會減少。時間一久，在不太複雜的文章中即使不畫（／）符號，也能一眼就理解整句的意義。

使用（／）符號來閱讀理解英語篇章
1. 能熟悉英文的句型和構造。
2. 可加速閱讀速度。

該方法對於需要邊聽理解的英文聽力也有很好的效果。
從現在開始，早日丟棄過去理解文章的習慣吧！

以直接閱讀理解的方式，重新閱讀《歌劇魅影》

從原文中摘錄一小段。以具有意義的詞組將文章做斷句區分，重新閱讀並做理解練習。

Sorelli, / one of the most important dancers at the Opera, / sat in her dressing room. //
莎蕾莉　　　歌劇院裡一位重要的舞者　　　坐在她的化妝室裡

She was getting ready / for the gala performance / for the two retiring managers of the Opera. //
她正準備好　　　為慶祝表演　　　為兩位劇院的退休經理

She was enjoying the peace and quiet, / but was suddenly interrupted / when a group of young girls came running into her room. //
她正享受放鬆平靜　　卻突然被打斷　　當一群年輕女孩跑進她房裡

The girls were talking excitedly. //
女孩們正興致勃勃地討論著

"The ghost! // We've seen him!" // one of them cried out. //
是幽靈　　　　我們看到他了！　　　其中一人喊道

"We've seen the ghost!" //
我們見到劇院魅影了！

Sorelli was very superstitious. //
莎蕾莉是非常迷信的

She was easily frightened / by stories of the ghost, / but she tried to be brave. //
她很容易受驚嚇　　　　被鬼故事　　　　　但她儘量拿出勇氣

"That's ridiculous!" / she told the girls. // "You are just being foolish." //
那太荒謬了！　　　她對女孩們說　　　妳們根本就是在說傻話

"No, no! // It's true. // We really all saw him," / the girls cried out. //
不，不！　這是真的　我們真的看見他了　　女孩們喊著

The chorus girls all claimed / to have seen him. //
合唱團的女孩全部宣稱　　　　見過他

In fact, / whenever anything unfortunate happened / in the building, / the girls always said, / "It was the ghost!" //
實際上　一旦不幸的事發生　　　　　　　在這棟建築物裡
女孩都會說　　　　一定是魅影做的！

For a while, / many didn't believe the girls. //
過了一會兒　　許多人不相信女孩們

Some thought / it was just their crazy imaginations. //
有些人認為　　　是她們瘋狂的想像

However, / this changed / when Joseph Buquet, one of the scene-shifters said, / "I saw the most terrible thing / in the corridor. //
不過　　　這改變了　　　當喬瑟夫・布克　　　其中一位布景人員說
我見到最嚇人的景象　　　　　在走廊

It was a figure / wearing a dress-suit. //
是一個人影　　穿著大禮服

At first, / I thought / he was from the audience. //
起初　　我以為　　他是從觀眾席來的

Then, / I looked at him / more closely. //
接著　　我看他　　　更仔細地

It had no face / – it was a skull! //
它沒有臉　　　是一個骷髏

The skin was yellow, / the eyes were black holes, / and the whole figure was terribly thin." //
皮膚是蠟黃的　　　　眼睛像黑洞　　　　　整個人瘦的很恐怖

Joseph was a very reliable man, / so no one doubted him. //
喬瑟夫是個非常值得信賴的人　　　所以沒有人懷疑他

Soon / everyone at the Opera / began to see strange things. //
很快地　　歌劇院裡的每個人　　開始見到奇怪的事

One of the firemen, Pampin, said, / "I went down into the cellars / yesterday morning. //
其中一位火夫・派平說　　　　　我走到地窖　　　　昨天清晨

When I was down there, / I saw the most horrifying thing. //
當我到那裡　　　　　我看到最恐怖的事物

117

Guide to Listening Comprehension

 When listening to the story, use some of the techniques shown below. If you take time to study some phonetic characteristics of English, listening will be easier.

Get in the flow of English.

English creates a rhythm formed by combinations of strong and weak stress intonations. Each word has its particular stress that combines with other words to form the overall pattern of stress or rhythm in a particular sentence.

When speaking and listening to English, it is essential to get in the flow of the rhythm of English. It takes a lot of practice to get used to such a rhythm. So, you need to start by identifying the stressed syllable in a word.

Listen for the strongly stressed words and phrases.

In English, key words and phrases that are essential to the meaning of a sentence are stressed louder. Therefore, pay attention to the words stressed with a higher pitch. When listening to an English recording for the first time, what matters most is to listen for a general understanding of what you hear. Do not try to hear every single word. Most of the unstressed words are articles or auxiliary verbs, which don't play an important role in the general context. At this level, you can ignore them.

Pay attention to liaisons.

In reading English, words are written with a space between them. There isn't such an obvious guide when it comes to listening to English. In oral English, there are many cases when the sounds of words are linked with adjacent words.

For instance, let's think about the phrase "**take off**," which can be used in "take off your clothes." "Take off your clothes" doesn't sound like [teɪk ɔːf] with each of the words completely and clearly separated from the others. Instead, it sounds as if almost all the words in context are slurred together, [ˈteɪkɔːf], for a more natural sound.

Shadow the voice of the native speaker.

Finally, you need to mimic the voice of the native speaker. Once you are sure you know how to pronounce all the words in a sentence, try to repeat them like an echo. Listen to the book again, but this time you should try a fun exercise while listening to the English.

This exercise is called "shadowing." The word "shadow" means a dark shade that is formed on a surface. When used as a verb, the word refers to the action of following someone or something like a shadow. In this exercise, pretend you are a parrot and try to shadow the voice of the native speaker.

Try to mimic the reader's voice by speaking at the same speed, with the same strong and weak stresses on words, and pausing or stopping at the same points.

Experts have already proven this technique to be effective. If you practice this shadowing exercise, your English speaking and listening skills will improve by leaps and bounds. While shadowing the native speaker, don't forget to pay attention to the meaning of each phrase and sentence.

Step 1 Listen to what you want to shadow many times. Start out by just trying to shadow a few words or a sentence.

 Step 2 Mimic the CD out loud. You can shadow everything the speaker says as if you are singing a round, or you also can speak simultaneously with the recorded voice of the native speaker.

 Step 3 As you practice more, try to shadow more. For instance, shadow a whole sentence or paragraph instead of just a few words.

Listening Guide

以下為《歌劇魅影》各章節的前半部。一開始若能聽清楚發音，之後就沒有聽力的負擔。先聽過摘錄的章節，之後再反覆聆聽括弧內單字的發音，並仔細閱讀各種發音的説明。以下都是以英語的典型發音為基礎，所做的簡易説明，即使這裡未提到的發音，也可以配合音檔反覆聆聽，如此一來聽力必能更上層樓。

Chapter One page 14–15 🎧41

Sorelli, (❶) ( ) ( ) most important dancers at the Opera, sat in her dressing room. She was getting ready for the gala performance for the two retiring managers of the Opera. She was enjoying the peace and quiet, but (❷) ( ) ( ) when a group of young girls came (❸) ( ) her room. The girls were talking excitedly.

"The ghost! (❹) ( ) ( )!" one of them cried out. "We've seen the ghost!"

Sorelli was very superstitious. She was easily (❺) ( ) stories of the ghost, but she tried to be brave.

"That's ridiculous!" she told the girls. "You are just being foolish."

"No, no! It's true. We really all saw him," the girls cried out. The chorus girls all claimed to have seen him.

❶ **one of the:** one 與 of 形成連音，發音為 [ˋwʌnəv]，of 的 -f 發 [v]
音，再與 the 結合後，整個連起來的發音為 [ˋwʌnͺəvðə]。one of the
是相當常見的詞組，不妨讓自己習慣聽此連音。

❷ **was suddenly interrupted:** was 和 suddenly 連在一起發音時，s
因前後重複故只發音一次，was 的發音較弱，重音放在 suddenly 上。
至於 interrupted 的 -nt- 連在一起發音，[t] 音常會被擺在不同的音節。

❸ **running into:** running 的重音在第一音節，該單字雖然有兩個 n，但
只發一次 [n] 的音，而字尾的 [ɪŋ] 音因為後面接的是極為相似的 in-，故
發音時迅速帶過，聽起來會像只發了一次 [iːn] 的音。

❹ **We've seen him:** We've 的 've 是 have 的縮寫，因附屬於主詞後，
故口語的發音微弱，不易聽出來，可由其後的 seen 判斷句型結構。
him 為句中的受詞，故 [h] 音會消失變成連音，通常以 h 開頭的代名詞
（him、his、her 等）或助動詞（have、had 等），依前後文迅速發音
時，[h] 音會迅速略過聽不清楚。

❺ **frightened by:** frightened 的重音在第一音節，單字的發音為
[fraɪtn̩d]，但因為後面接了 by，故原本的 [d] 音會迅速略過，聽的時候
必須注意前後文來判斷動詞的時態。

In fact, whenever (❶) (   ) happened in the building, the girls always said, "It was the ghost!"

For a while, many didn't believe the girls. Some thought it (❷) (   ) (   ) crazy imaginations. However, this changed when Joseph Buquet, one of the scene-shifters, said, "I saw the most terrible thing in the corridor. It was a figure wearing a dress-suit. At first, I thought he was from the audience. Then, I (❸) (   ) him more closely. It had no face – (❹) (   ) (   ) (   )! The skin was yellow, the eyes were black holes, and the whole figure was terribly thin."

Joseph was a very reliable man, so no one (❺) (   ). Soon everyone at the Opera began to see strange things. One of the firemen, Pampin, said, "I (❻) (   ) into the cellars yesterday morning. When I was down there, I saw the most horrifying thing. I saw a head of fire coming toward me! It was so clear. I remember it very distinctly. It had a head of fire, but the head had no body at all!"

❶ anything unfortunate: unfortunate 的重音在第二音節，所以在日常會話中，un- 的音調下降，幾乎聽不見，另外類似的字首像是 -in、-a 都會出現同樣的情況，故在口語對話時應由前後文判斷。

❷ was just their: was 的 [s] 音會輕聲略過，幾乎聽不出來，而 just 字尾的 [t] 音消失，與 their 的 [ð] 音連在一起發音，整句話的重音放在 just 上。

❸ looked at: looked 和 at 連在一起發音，-ed 發無聲的 [t] 音，兩個單字連在一起的發音會變成 [ˋlukˌtæt]。

❹ it was a skull: skull 中 s 後的 k 發音為有聲子音，通常 s 後若接著 [t]、[p]、[k] 等子音，這些子音會由無聲轉變為有聲發音，skin 就是另一個例子。

❺ doubted him: doubted 的重音在第一音節，-ed 發 [id] 的音，當 doubted 與 him 連在一起時，him 的 [h] 通常發很輕的音，整句的發音聽起來就像 [daʊtidim]。doubted 的 b 不發音，而 t 的前後都是母音，會讓 t 的發音轉為類似 [d] 的有聲音。

❻ went down: went 的字尾 t 與 down 連在一起，[t] 音會迅速略過，聽起來像沒有發音。

4

Listening Comprehension

🎧 43 **A** Listen to the CD and fill in the blanks.

1 Joseph was a very _____ man, so no one doubted him.

2 Sorelli looked in the _____, but she saw nothing.

3 Someone found his _____ in the cellar. He was _____!

4 But it was decided that it was a "_____ _____."

5 Raoul was very soon to begin a _____ in the navy.

6 Christine, I am the boy who long ago rescued your _____ from the sea.

7 He felt a sharp pain in his _____, and he could feel his heart _____.

🎧 44 **B** Write down the sentences you hear and write "T" for True, "F" for False.

T F 1 ....

T F 2 ....

T F 3 ....

T F 4 ....

T F 5 ....

45

C Listen to the CD, write down the questions and choose the correct answer.

1 _____?

    (a) Because she was going to marry Erik in a month.

    (b) Because Raoul was going to leave for navy.

    (c) Because she didn't love Raoul as much as Erik.

2 _____?

    (a) Because she really couldn't recognize him.

    (b) Because she wanted to make fun of him.

    (c) Because she knew Erik would be very jealous of him.

46

D Listen to the CD and write down the sentences. Rearrange the sentences in chronological order.

① ....

② ....

③ ....

④ ....

⑤ ....

_____ ⇨ _____ ⇨ _____ ⇨ _____ ⇨ _____

Translation

作者簡介

p. 4　1868 年，法國小說家卡斯頓‧勒胡出生於巴黎一戶富裕人家中。勒胡取得大學法律學位後，卻將繼承的大筆遺產揮霍於飲酒賭博，就在蕩盡家產之際，他開始了報紙記者的生涯。1890 年代，勒胡以記者的身分走訪世界，替法國報紙報導全球各大事件及歷險，包括 1905 年的俄國革命。

而自 1900 年代初期，他開始專心致志於寫作，大部分是推理小說。《黃色房間之謎》，講述業餘偵探精彩的密室推理故事，是他第一部大受歡迎的小說，也讓勒胡一舉成為知名作家。

卡斯頓‧勒胡以他記者生涯經驗為靈感、佐以獨特的新聞寫作風格，創作了多部小說。他的小說令讀者感受到無懈可擊的邏輯，彷彿一同身歷犯罪情境，抽絲剝繭、解開迷霧。《歌劇魅影》也是勒胡的代表作之一，讓他贏得「法國當代最佳推理小說家」的美譽。勒胡逝世後，《歌劇魅影》被改編為多部舞台劇與電影，是他享譽國際的成功代表作。

故事簡介

p. 5　《歌劇魅影》的故事場景在巴黎歌劇院，漫天謠言敘述一名鬼魂引發了劇院一連串的恐怖事件。名叫艾瑞克的魅影，用面具遮住了他布滿疤痕的臉，住在巴黎歌劇院地底墓穴中的一處。艾瑞克愛上了美麗的歌劇名伶克莉絲汀，並教她唱歌。

一天，克莉絲汀的青梅竹馬勞爾出現，艾瑞克變得異常妒忌。就在一場歌劇的開幕之夜，艾瑞克擄走了克莉絲汀，帶她走過地下墓穴，來到一座地底湖邊。勞爾冒著生命危險，潛進地窖拯救他的青梅竹馬。雖然克莉絲汀愛的是勞爾，但她對魅影卻充滿同情，即便在她撕下他面具、見到他幾近毀容的駭人臉龐，她仍給歌劇魅影誠摯的一吻，於是，他得到了救贖。

最後，魅影放走了克莉絲汀與勞爾，從此消失，因為他明白自己對克莉絲汀的愛，永遠不可能開花結果。

如同《美女與野獸》、《鐘樓怪人》及《金剛》，美麗女主角與醜陋男主角間心碎的愛情，一直是西方文學常見的故事主軸。在魅影的愛情故事中，作者用精準、栩栩如生且充滿懸疑的鋪陳，完滿了一部推理小說能成功的所有元素，也深深贏得了讀者的心。時序到了二十一世紀，《歌劇魅影》仍廣受各地大眾喜愛，並在不同的藝術媒介有著各式充滿創意的改編。

p. 12-13

艾瑞克（魅影）

我生來便長得一副嚇人的臉孔，沒有人會愛上我的外表，包括我母親在內。雖然我的外表醜陋，老天卻賦予我美好的嗓音與極高的智慧。我建造了歌劇院，裡面有無數的暗門與秘密通道，歌劇院裡的人大都還以為我是幽靈。

克莉絲汀

我是歌劇院裡的歌手，我的聲音並不完美，因此在劇院裡我只是一名普通的歌手。某天夜裡，艾瑞克來到我面前，調教我唱歌。他希望我能愛他，但是我做不到，我心另有所屬。

勞爾

我是個即將加入法國皇家海軍的青年，我在年輕時愛上了克莉絲汀，但是後來我卻與她失去聯繫。某一天夜晚，我在巴黎見到她在歌劇院裡演唱，在這次的邂逅中，我得知了她的遭遇，也明白她還是深愛著我的！

波斯人

過去我曾經是波斯的警察。我認識艾瑞克已經很長一段時間了，我對他的遭遇深感同情，但是我知道有時候他是個危險分子，因此我定居巴黎，隨時監視他的一舉一動。

[第一章] 劇院魅影

`p. 14-15` 莎蕾莉，歌劇院裡舉足輕重的舞者，坐在她的化妝室裡，正打點好一切，準備為即將退休的兩位劇院經理獻上一場表演盛宴。就在她放鬆平靜的這一刻，卻被突然闖進她房裡的一群年輕女孩給打斷了，這些女孩們正興致勃勃地討論著。

「是幽靈！我們看到他了！」其中一人高喊道，「我們見到劇院魅影了！」

莎蕾莉非常迷信，就連說個小小的鬼故事都能把她嚇得半死，但她還是壯壯膽子。「別胡扯了！」她對女孩們說道，「真是一派胡言。」

「不，才不是呢！是真的，我們大家的確都看見了。」女孩子們連忙喊道。

這些歌舞女郎全都聲稱見過魅影。實際上，只要這棟建築物裡發生任何一點不好的事，這些女孩都會說：「一定是魅影做的！」

`p. 16-17` 一段時間之後，許多人不再相信這些女孩所說的話，直當是她們自己在那裡胡思亂想。但這一切在喬瑟夫・布克，這位布景人員開口後就改變了，他說：「我曾經在走廊上見過最恐怖的東西，那是個穿著大禮服的身影。一開始我以為他只是觀眾，但當我靠近，仔細一看，卻發現這個人竟然沒有臉——一個骷髏頭！他皮膚蠟黃，眼睛是兩個黑洞，整個身影瘦得嚇人。」喬瑟夫是個老實人，所以沒人懷疑他說的話。

沒多久，歌劇院裡的每個人都遇到一些奇奇怪怪的事。一位火夫派平說：「昨天早上我去地窖，我一走到那兒就遇到生平見過最可怕的東西，我看到一個冒著火的人頭朝我飛過來！它的確就在那裡，我到現在還記得一清二楚，那是個冒著火的人頭，頭的下面完全沒有身體！」

p. 18-19 在莎蕾莉的化妝室裡，女孩子們還繼續說著這樁事，「我們真的看到他了！」一名女孩很篤定地說，「就是魅影沒錯！」

化妝室裡突然變得異常安靜，只聽得見女孩們恐懼的喘息聲。其中一個女孩把耳朵貼在門上，聽著門外的動靜，臉色突然變得蒼白。

「你們聽！」她驚恐地低聲說。

門外傳來一陣沙沙聲，然後又突然靜止下來。

莎蕾莉緩緩走到門邊，對著門外問：「誰……是誰……在外面？」

沒有人回答。

「有人在我門口嗎？」

「有啊，有啊！」其中一位叫梅格的女孩說，「我們都聽到有聲音，但是千萬別開門，妳一開門他就會進來了。」但莎蕾莉沒理睬她的話。

莎蕾莉總會隨身帶著刀，她從腳踝上的刀鞘裡取出一把刀，緊握在手裡，再一邊小心翼翼地把門打開。女孩子們都縮在房間的角落裡。莎蕾莉朝走廊瞧了瞧，什麼也沒看到，「外面什麼也沒有。」她告訴這些女孩。

p. 20-21 莎蕾莉鼓起勇氣說：「大家冷靜一點，沒有人真正看過魅影。」

「可是我們看過他，加百列也看過他。」又一個女孩補充道。

「加百列，歌舞團長？」莎蕾莉問，「他說了什麼？」

「他在經理的辦公室裡，當時那個奇怪的波斯人……，妳應該知道他吧？也進了經理辦公室。」

「我知道，」莎蕾莉回答，「我知道那個波斯人。」

133

每個歌劇院裡的人都認識那個波斯人，女孩子們都很怕他。

「接著怎麼了？」莎蕾莉問道。

「加百列一看到波斯人，突然發狂，衝出辦公室。他不小心在樓梯間滑了一跤，從樓梯上跌了下來。媽媽和我是在樓梯下面發現他的，他當時全身都是鮮血和傷痕。後來，他告訴我們他當時為什麼會那麼害怕，原來，他往波斯人的肩膀身後望過去時，看到了一個鬼影，就在波斯人的身後！加百列真是嚇壞了！」

「那個鬼影看起來是什麼樣子的？」莎蕾莉很想知道。

「他身穿著大禮服，就跟喬瑟夫·布克說的一樣，而他的頭，就像是一個骷髏！」女孩形容道。

p. 22–23　「我母親說布克太多嘴了。」梅格靜靜說著。

梅格的母親，季蕊夫人也在歌劇院裡工作，負責管理劇院的包廂。

「妳母親是怎麼跟妳說的？」女孩們問梅格。

「她說魅影不喜歡別人提到他，」梅格緩緩回答，「像第五號包廂啊，你們知道是我母親管理的，五號包廂是魅影專屬的座位，」她對大家說，「劇院有表演的時候他就會在那裡，其他人都不能過去。」

「妳母親見過他嗎？」女孩們問她。

「沒有，」梅格解釋道，「根本沒有人能看見他。那些說什麼他穿著大禮服，什麼臉長得像骷髏，什麼冒火的人頭，根本都是在胡扯。我母親從沒見過他，只有當他在包廂裡的時候聽過他說話，把節目表拿給他。」

女孩們面面相覷，梅格所說的，聽起來就像在鬼扯淡。

p. 24–25　這時化妝室的門突然被打開，一個女人衝了進來，她睜大雙眼，充滿了恐懼。「喬瑟夫·布克！」她氣喘吁吁地喊著，「他死了！有人在地窖裡發現了他的屍體，他被吊死了！」

房間裡的人莫不是一臉驚恐。

「是魅影做的。」梅格話一脫口，就立刻用手摀住嘴，想收回剛才說的話，生怕自己也會被魅影給找上了。

「那不是我說的，」她說，「我什麼也沒說。」但大家都很同意她的說法，「沒錯，一定就是魅影做的。」

事情發生後，警方對此展開調查，但是調查的結果卻顯示這是一起「沒有外力介入的自殺事件」。但接下來奇怪的事情發生了，喬瑟夫用來上吊的繩子突然不見了！經理的說法是：「一定是有人把它拿回去做紀念了，這件事情總會水落石出的。」

p. 28-29

認識故事場景：巴黎歌劇院

卡斯頓‧勒胡所寫的這個故事，背景是設定在世界知名的巴黎歌劇院。許多讀者以為，故事裡所描述的巨大舞台、知名的大吊燈、地下秘密通道，甚至歌劇院下方的湖泊，根本子虛烏有的。但是實際上，在巴黎歌劇院裡，這些都確有其物！

劇院裡的座位可以容納兩千多名觀眾，在劇院的後牆上，每一層樓都有數個包廂，而勒胡所寫的五號包廂，這個魅影的私人座位，也的確存在，包廂的位置就鄰近劇院出口。

劇院裡也的確掛著巨型吊燈。西元 1896 年，吊燈在表演時突然掉落下來，砸死了坐在第 13 號座位的觀眾，很多人認為這應該就是勒胡寫下這篇故事的靈感。

巴黎歌劇院底下的確有一座湖，這是為了支撐並固定舞台的重量而鑿的。不過這座湖並不大，湖中央也沒有小島可以作為魅影的藏身之所。這一點，應該是勒胡小說中與真實的巴黎歌劇院唯一不相符的地方吧。

[第二章] 房裡的回聲

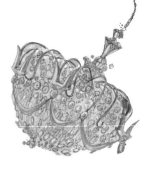

p. 30–31　當晚的表演空前成功，是歌劇院經營以來最出色的一場演出，觀眾不停地喊著「安可」、「安可」！每一位舞者、作曲家、演唱者的表現，都出奇地協調，讓整場演出達到超群的水準。

其中，又屬克莉絲汀‧戴依的演出最為耀眼。過去她並不是劇院裡最出色的歌手，但今晚，她猶如一朵綻放的花朵，歌聲充滿了激情與力量。當演到《浮士德》那一段在地牢中的最後三重唱時，聽眾更是聽得如痴如醉。

演出到最後，觀眾完全為之瘋狂，而投入全副心神的克莉絲汀更是昏厥過去，被送回了化妝室。

p. 32–33　在觀眾席中，有一名男子，特別專注地聽著克莉絲汀的演唱。

他是一名年輕的子爵，勞爾‧夏尼。他與兄長菲利普‧夏尼伯爵一起來觀賞這晚的表演。

菲利普，四十一歲，他在父母過世後，便與姊姊和一位姨媽一起將這個年紀甚小的弟弟撫養長大。菲利普很以弟弟勞爾為榮，如今勞爾已經是一位有為又健康的青年了。也由於姨媽是一名海軍官員的遺孀，勞爾因此對海洋產生了一種嚮往。很快他就要展開他的海軍職業生涯。趁他還在巴黎時，菲利普決定帶他去市中心看一些藝術表演，而欣賞歌劇便是其中的一項。

那一晚，在表演途中，勞爾對哥哥說：「她看起來不太舒服，像是要昏倒了。她以前不會這樣子的，我得去看看她。」

p. 34–35　勞爾走進克莉絲汀的房間，劇院的醫生早他一步抵達。克莉絲汀此時正好甦醒了過來。勞爾便問：「醫師，是不是請大家離開房間比較好一點？」

「沒錯，」醫師同意，「大家都出去吧！每個人都出去！」醫師大聲說道。

只剩下勞爾、醫師、女僕和克莉絲汀留在房裡。

克莉絲汀見到勞爾時問道：「先生，請問您是哪位？」

勞爾回答：「克莉絲汀，我就是很久以前幫妳從海裡找回圍巾的那個小男孩啊！」克莉絲汀看看在竊笑的醫師和女僕，勞爾感到很難為情，便說道：「如果妳不記得了，我希望能私下與妳談一談。」

「等我身體好點了，我會再請你過來，」克莉絲汀說：「請你們都先出去吧，今晚我想要靜一靜。」

p. 36–37 這時，整個劇院裡已經空無一人。勞爾在走廊上等著，他看到女僕從克莉絲汀的房間走出來，問道：「克莉絲汀現在怎麼樣了？」

女僕笑笑地說：「她現在覺得好多了，但是她想獨處，請你先別去打擾她。」

勞爾突然想到：「她想獨處？她會不會其實是想支開其他人，私下與我交談？」

他悄悄走到克莉絲汀的門邊，正想要敲門時，卻突然傳來一個男人的聲音。

「克莉絲汀，妳一定要愛我！」

克莉絲汀哭著說道：「你怎能說這些話？我只為你一個人歌唱啊！」

勞爾覺得整顆心被刺穿了，胸口一陣劇烈的刺痛，甚至能聽見自己的心臟在砰砰作響。這時，他又聽到那個男人的聲音：「妳累了嗎？」

「我已經把靈魂交給你，如今我根本不算活著了。」克莉絲汀用極為哀傷的嗓音回答。

「妳的靈魂很美，我很感激妳，那是最美好的一份禮物。」

（略）

p. 38　這時勞爾決定先躲在暗處等。他心中五味雜陳，尤其是對克莉絲汀的愛，交織著對陌生男子的恨。

「我要知道讓我痛恨的那個人到底是誰。」他想。

沒過多久，克莉絲汀走出房間，她離開時沒有鎖上房門。一等到她走遠了，勞爾便走進她的房間，把房門關上。房間裡一團漆黑。

「你是誰？」他高聲問道，「你躲在哪裡？現在就站出來，你這個懦夫！」他劃了根火柴，把煤燈點上，將整個房間檢查了一遍，卻沒見到任何身影，令人非常的困惑。

「難道有秘密通道？」他想著，「還是我自己發瘋了？」

p. 40–41　那天稍晚，有一場為兩位退休的劇院經理所舉辦的晚宴，在大家都玩得很盡興時，卻突然出現一個陌生的身影。他穿著正式的套裝，臉看起來卻像極了骷髏。

「那是劇院幽靈，」人們竊竊私語，「歌劇院裡的魅影。」

這時，詭異的身影高聲說：「喬瑟夫·布克的死並不是自殺。」

在場的每一個人，特別是劇院經理，全都震驚不已，但那抹身影卻又突然消失不見。

過了一會兒，兩位退休經理坐在那兒與新任的兩名經理李察、莫查寧談話。

「我們會盡量幫忙，」他們說，「現在我們要做的就是談談劇院幽靈的事。」

經理李察笑了出來，他想，「這簡直是個大笑話。」不過他還是問：「他這麼做是為了什麼？」

其中一位退休經理交給他一份文件，上面寫著：

> 歌劇院經理每月必須支付魅影兩萬法郎，亦即每
> 年二十四萬法郎的薪資。
> 每當劇院有表演時，依然必須為魅影保留第五號
> 包廂。

p. 42–43 兩位新來的經理相視大笑，根本不把魅影當一回事，他們覺得這不過是一場無聊的惡作劇罷了。但是過了幾天，他們又收到一封以紅色字體書寫的奇怪信件，上面的筆跡很像小孩所寫的字，信裡寫到：

> 你們沒有把第五號包廂留給我！
> 再不把包廂還給我，很快你們就會遇上大麻煩。
>
> 　　　　　　　　　　劇院魅影

隔天，他們又收到一封同樣以紅色字體書寫的信，寫著：

> 你們必須支付我兩萬法郎，否則後果
> 請自行負責！
>
> 　　　　　　　　　　劇院魅影

新來的經理說：「這一定是以前的經理寫的，他們想拿劇院魅影來開我們玩笑，我們不用理會。」

不多久，他們便將第五號包廂的票賣出去。

p. 44–45 好幾天過去了，歌劇院裡什麼事也沒發生，但就在某個晚上，坐在第五號包廂的觀眾表現出奇怪的行徑，台上正在演出，他們卻在包廂裡大笑大叫。

兩位經理問警衛：「昨晚第五號包廂發生什麼事了？」

警衛回答：「包廂裡的觀眾說，他們一直聽到某個聲音說著『第五號包廂已經有人坐了！』接著他們便開始做出一些嚇人的舉動。」

「包廂的管理人又怎麼說？」經理繼續問道。

「她說那是劇院裡的魅影。」警衛回答。

「現在就去把她找來！」他們命令道。

包廂的管理員，季蕊夫人過來了。

「那是劇院魅影，經理，」她說，「他很生氣你們沒有為他保留包廂，沒有付他薪水。」

「他和妳說過話嗎？」劇院經理問她。

「當然，他叫我拿腳凳給他。」她回答。

兩名經理突然爆笑出聲，但這位女士可是很嚴肅認真的。兩位經理於是決定將她解雇。

[第三章] 音樂天使

p. 48–49 在那一晚的慶祝表演之後，克莉絲汀就一直沒再出現，似乎她就這麼憑空消失了。勞爾寫了好幾封信給克莉絲汀，詢問是否能去拜訪她，卻一直毫無回音，但是不久後，克莉絲汀卻寫了一封信到他家。

先生：

我並沒有忘記那個為我到海裡找圍巾的小男孩。我想我今天應該在前往鄉下之前，寫一封信給您。明天是我父親的祭日，他生前很喜歡您。他與他的小提琴就埋葬在我們小時候一起玩耍的地方。

克莉絲汀

勞爾決定尾隨克莉絲汀到她下榻的鄉間旅館。第二天，他在漫長的火車旅程上，兒時的記憶一幕幕湧現。

p. 50 勞爾小時候，就認識了克莉絲汀和她的父親戴依先生。當時在一個小鎮上，勞爾遇見正在演唱而由父親小提琴伴奏的克莉絲汀時，便愛上她了，那天的風很大，強風將她的圍巾吹落海中，勞爾跳進水裡，幫她拿回圍巾，從此他們就成了好友。

他們在一起度過了許多快樂的日子，克莉絲汀的父親對他們說了許多有趣的故事，其中他講了一個「音樂天使」的故事。他說，只有在見過音樂天使之後，人才可能唱出或是演奏出完美的音樂。

之後許多年過去了，那天當勞爾在歌劇院見到克莉絲汀時，舊時對她的愛意又回到心頭。

p. 52-53 當勞爾抵達鄉下的小旅館時，克莉絲汀已經在那兒等著他了。「我很高興你果真來了。」她說。

「我不明白，為什麼那一晚在化妝室裡妳要假裝不認識我？」他問。

克莉絲汀沒有回答。

勞爾氣憤地說：「因為有另外一個男人，我聽到他的聲音，他就在妳房裡。」

「你說這話是什麼意思？」她問道，表情看起來似乎有些驚慌。

「我聽到妳說：『我只為你一個人歌唱。』接著妳還說：『今晚我已經把靈魂交給你！』」勞爾說。

「你還聽到了些什麼？」她問。

「他還說：『妳必須要愛我。』克莉絲汀，他是誰？」

「告訴我你聽到的一切。」她堅持道。

勞爾說出那一晚他聽到了什麼，以及做了什麼。

「那是音樂天使，」克莉絲汀說，「你聽到的那個聲音，已經為我上了三個月的音樂課了。」

勞爾並不相信音樂天使的故事，他覺得很疑惑。

p. 54 那天晚上，克莉絲汀離開旅館，勞爾在暗夜裡偷偷跟著她走到她父親的墳前。這是個非常奇特的夜晚，四下一片死寂，整個墓園籠罩著層層薄霧。不過他仍可以看見克莉絲汀跪在她父親的墓前。

這時勞爾聽見一陣奇異的樂聲從空中飄送下來，他正準備往前走，卻見到幾道骷髏般的身影從他面前晃過，他嚇得往後跳了幾步，不期撞到了身後的某個人。那人披著長斗蓬，渾身散發著邪氣，這時他露出臉，一個骷髏般的臉龐，蠟黃的皮膚，凹陷的雙眼。勞爾見狀，旋即昏倒在地上。

p. 56–57 就在這期間，歌劇院裡的兩個經理正在檢查第五號包廂，他們沒有發現任何不尋常的地方，但是過了幾天，他們又收到另一封信，信上寫下了四項要求：

1. 把第五號包廂給我。
2. 今晚必須讓克莉絲汀‧戴依飾演瑪格麗特的角色。
3. 我的包廂管理人必須再回到工作崗位上。
4. 每月支付我兩萬法郎。

如果做不到以上要求，今晚的《浮士德》演出時，將會有災難發生。

經理看了信之後氣憤不已，他們對這些惡作劇已經非常厭煩了。但麻煩的事不止一樁，那天晚上，馬伕跑來辦公室說道：「有一匹馬被偷了，我想是劇院魅影做的，我看到一道黑影在黑夜中把馬騎走。」

p. 58–59 同一天晚上，歌劇院的頭號女高音，卡洛塔，坐在專屬化妝室裡讀著一封信，上面寫著：

> 親愛的卡洛塔：
>
> 別在今晚的《浮士德》劇中演唱。
> 如果妳上台表演，比死還慘的悲劇將會降臨在妳身上。

卡洛塔對著信想了又想，她很緊張，但是如果她今晚不上台演唱，克莉絲汀就會上台表演，她嫉妒克莉絲汀的歌聲，所以還是決定上台。

當天晚上《浮士德》一劇讓歌劇院席席滿座，卡洛塔一開口演唱，便忘記了信上所提的一切威脅，但駭人的事緊接著發生了。就在她唱到一半時，突然發出一聲像青蛙一樣的呱叫聲，令現場頓然鴉雀無聲。

這時兩位經裡的身後，傳來一個聲音說道：「她的歌聲會讓大吊燈掉下來。」

他們聽了驚恐不已，抬頭看著大吊燈，只見吊燈直直掉下落在觀眾席中，砸死了一個女人。

p. 62–63

認識故事：歌劇魅影的電影與舞台版本

小說一開始出版的時候，沒有人想到勒胡的小說《歌劇魅影》會受到這麼長久的喜愛。當時，許多評論家提出小說中的諸多缺點，並認為它只是一部低級的鬼故事，不過，勒胡將鬼故事放在巨大神秘的歌劇院裡，確實是電影和戲劇的絕佳題材。

1927 年，電影版初次問世，由朗錢尼主演。在這之前，勒胡已有其他作品被拍成電影，但《歌劇魅影》卻是最賣座的一部。

接下來的數十年間，有更多重拍的版本，也有好幾齣舞台劇出現。最著名的舞台劇版本，莫過於安德烈‧洛伊‧韋伯在 1988 年所推出的版本。韋伯回歸勒胡原著所描述的故事，但把故事中幾個重大的瑕疵刪除，他的創作讓《歌劇魅影》成為世界知名的音樂劇，並在全球各地上演超過 7,000 次。

[第四章] 居於歌劇院底的人

`p. 64–65` 在那場意外過後，克莉絲汀又再度失蹤。勞爾想找她，但找不到。某天晚上，他正要走回家時，竟看到克莉絲汀就坐在一輛馬車裡。

「克莉絲汀，克莉絲汀。」他喊道。

接著他聽到一個男人的聲音：「繼續走！」當這個聲音一說完，馬車便離開了。

勞爾想：「克莉絲汀真的愛上別人了。」

第二天清晨，勞爾接到一封信。

親愛的勞爾：

後天歌劇院將會舉辦一場化妝舞會，穿著白色的長袍來參加，我會在午夜與你見面。

克莉絲汀

勞爾萬般期待，他興奮地讀著信，決定去參加化妝舞會，但他又想：「誰是音樂天使？克莉絲汀愛上他了嗎？還是她根本就被他囚禁？」這些不確定感讓他心裡忐忑不安。

`p. 66–67` 歌劇院舉辦的化妝舞會是一場盛大的饗宴，巴黎的富豪名人全都來參加。勞爾來到舞會，接近午夜時分時，一名戴著黑色面具的人來到他面前，那是克莉絲汀，她示意勞爾跟著她。

他們穿過人群，勞爾看見一個高大的男人，穿著一身紅衣，戴著寬大的帽子和一個骷髏面具，許多人聚集在他面前，勞爾看見他長袍上的幾個字：「不要碰我！我是紅色死神！」

勞爾跟著克莉絲汀來到劇院包廂。她說：「別擔心，他不知道我們在這裡。」

但是勞爾的視線可以看見外面的走廊，紅色死神也正走向走廊！

「他過來了！他到走廊上了！」勞爾說。

「誰？」克莉絲汀問。

「紅色死神！妳的音樂天使！我要去見他，摘下他臉上的面具。」勞爾回答。

「求求你！不要，千萬別這麼做！」克莉絲汀喊著，擋住他的去路，「如果你愛我就別這麼做！」

勞爾一時妒火中燒。

「妳愛他，是嗎？」他吼道，「妳走！我不會阻止妳，但是我恨妳，克莉絲汀，妳這麼惡劣地對待我，前一秒妳看似愛我，下一秒卻又不愛了。妳走吧！」

克莉絲汀看起來是那麼悲傷。

p. 68–69 「總有一天你會明白的，」她喃喃說著，「我該走了，請不要跟著我。」接著她離開勞爾往走廊去。

化妝舞會還沒結束，但是勞爾已經不想再回去，此刻他沒有飲酒作樂的心情，他只是在歌劇院裡四處遊蕩走動。

他痛苦地走著，發現自己正走向克莉絲汀的化妝室。他把門推開走進去，過了一會兒，克莉絲汀也走了進來，她將黑色的手套脫下，勞爾見到她手上戴著一枚金戒指。

「結婚戒指？」他想，「是誰給她的？紅色死神？」

克莉絲汀坐下，將臉埋在手中嘆息道：「可憐的艾瑞克！可憐的艾瑞克！」

「艾瑞克？」勞爾納悶，「誰是艾瑞克？」

突然間，勞爾聽到遠處傳來一陣歌聲。他凝神聆聽，發現歌聲越來越近，沒過多久，歌聲聽起來就好像是在房間裡頭的。

「是艾瑞克！」她叫著。

「你遲到了！」歌聲依然持續著，唱著《羅蜜歐與茱莉葉》劇中的「婚禮之夜」，那真是世界上最美的歌聲。

p. 70–71　勞爾突然明白克莉絲汀的歌聲為何進步神速了。克莉絲汀起身走向鏡子，勞爾跟在她身後。他突然感覺一陣冷風襲來，整個房間彷彿開始天旋地轉似地。他不知道到底發生了什麼事，當一切平靜下來，克莉絲汀已經從房裡消失了！

勞爾回到歌劇院時，才又看到克莉絲汀。克莉絲汀似乎很高興見到他。

「勞爾，我很高興再見到你！」她表示，「你什麼時候會離開這裡加入海軍？」

「再過一個月。」勞爾回答，克莉絲汀瞬間看起來非常難過。

「就是說，再過一個月，我們就要永遠分開了。」她十分落寞地說道。

「但我們還是可以真誠相待，還是可以對彼此忠實。」勞爾說。

克莉絲汀雙眸含著淚水回答：「我是無法嫁給你的，勞爾。」這時她傷感的語調突然轉變，「不過我們可以訂婚一個月，就算是我們之間的小秘密。」

「好啊！」勞爾同意道，「我們就訂婚一個月吧！」

p. 72–73　他們對彼此許下承諾後，在歌劇院度過好多天開心的日子。這棟建築物非常壯觀，克莉絲汀帶著勞爾參觀了每一個角落。有一天，當他們走過一扇天窗活板門時，勞爾說：「妳帶我看遍了整座巴黎歌劇院，但是卻沒有去過地下通道，我們一起去看看吧！」

克莉絲汀臉色忽然轉為蒼白，一臉驚恐。

「不要，我們別下去那兒，那裡是他的地方。」她說。

「喔，所以艾瑞克就住在那裡，對不對？」他問。

克莉絲汀走開幾步說道：「我不想談這件事，我們能在一起的時間很短，我們何不好好享受這段時光？」勞爾回頭再看看那扇門，門已經關上了。

「是他關的，是不是？」他問。

克莉絲汀沒有回答，只是默默地走開，勞爾在後面追著她：「妳聽我說，如果妳很怕他，我可以幫妳，我可以帶妳去一個他找不到的地方。」

她滿懷希望地望著勞爾。

p. 74–75 克莉絲汀抓著勞爾的手，帶他來到歌劇院屋頂。

「我們在這裡談話很安全，」她說，「我要把一切都告訴你。勞爾，你知道我並沒有一副很好的歌喉，但是某天晚上，牆壁裡傳來一陣好美的歌聲，我問他是不是音樂天使，他回答是。於是我和他成了好朋友，他教我怎麼改善我的音色，因為他，我的歌聲變得和以前不同。接著那一天，我在觀眾席上看到你，我對你舊情復燃，我就對音樂天使提到你，結果他突然吃醋起來，說我必須在你和他之間做選擇，我很害怕會失去他的教導，所以我那天在化妝室裡就假裝不認識你。」

「我懂了。」勞爾說。

克莉絲汀繼續說道：「那天晚上當大吊燈掉下來的時候，我很害怕，接著我回到化妝室，但化妝裡的擺設都不一樣了。我走到鏡子面前，鏡子卻開始移動，接著我就發現自己處在一個完全陌生的地方了。」

勞爾心想：「沒錯，就跟我躲在化妝室裡的情況一樣。」

p. 76–77 「當時四周一片黑暗，然後有某個人走到我身邊，將我拉到一匹馬上，於是我們就騎著馬走在歌劇院的地窖，一直走到劇院下方的湖泊，他帶我坐上一艘船，划向湖心的一處住所。到了那裡就看得比較清楚，但是他戴著一個造型奇怪的深色面具，他帶我坐在沙發上，叫我不要害怕，並且很溫柔地對我這麼說：『我不是音樂天使，我叫艾瑞克，我是人，不是什麼幽靈。』他說：『請妳留在這兒陪我五天，我很喜歡妳，五天後我就會讓妳走，只要妳答應永遠不看我的臉，我保證一定會讓妳走。』」

「但是我之後卻做了一件蠢事，我把他的面具拿下來看了他骷髏般的臉，凹陷的雙眼，他對我大吼：『妳看了我的臉，就永遠不能離開這裡了，因為妳再也不會回來見我，所以我決不會讓妳離開。』接著他就把我一個人留在那裡。」

p. 78–79 「接下來又發生了什麼事？」勞爾問。

「我決定表現出根本不怕他的長相，雖然他的臉的確把我嚇壞了，但我很想離開那裡，我知道那是離開的唯一辦法。最後他總算放我走了。」

「妳還有再回去過嗎？」勞爾問。

「有。」她回答。

「為什麼？」這名年輕人問。

「因為我為他感到難過，他很寂寞，每個見到他的臉的人都怕他。」她回答。

就在這時候，他們抬頭看見那個嚇人的身影正朝他們這兒過來，克莉絲汀拉住勞爾的手，跑向屋頂的另一端，驚恐地走下樓梯。

[第五章] 克莉絲汀失蹤！

p. 82–83 克莉絲汀和勞爾跑遍整個歌劇院，想要躲開艾瑞克。突然間，一個人擋住他們的去路，他的膚色很深，身上穿著中東國家的服飾。

「從那邊走。」他說，他們依照男人所指的方向走去，最後來到克莉絲汀的房間裡。

「那個人是誰？」勞爾問。

「他是波斯人，他一直都待在歌劇院裡。」她回答。

「克莉絲汀，我要妳和我一起離開，像這樣住在這裡簡直太荒謬了。」勞爾說。

「今天不行，」她回答，「我答應艾瑞克要在明天的演出中為他獻唱，我一定得做到，等表演完畢我會和你一起離開。」

接著他們便討論隔天晚上逃跑的計畫。

p. 84–85 第二天，勞爾便為當晚逃跑的計畫做準備，他訂了一輛馬車，會在演出結束時候在歌劇院外。

那晚歌劇院座無虛席，每個人都是為了來聽克莉絲汀演唱。她一開始非常緊張，後來才漸漸放鬆下來，獻上她最精采的演出，全場觀眾為之瘋狂，站起身報以最熱烈的掌聲。但此時燈光卻突然熄滅，劇院裡陷入一片漆黑，接著傳來一陣尖叫聲——是女人的尖叫聲。

經理迅速把燈打開，但克莉絲汀卻失去了蹤影。觀眾席傳來一陣陣嘈雜的私語，勞爾非常擔心，立刻衝到經理辦公室，想要知道發生了什麼事。

就在他正要進門之時，一隻手拍了拍他的肩膀，是那個波斯人。

「別跟任何人談到艾瑞克。」他警告地說道，接著他將手指放在唇上，示意勞爾保守秘密。

p. 86–87 勞爾走進經理辦公室，裡面聚集了許多人，包括一名警探。他們全都狐疑地看著勞爾，警探問他：「你和戴依小姐常常在一起，對吧？」

「沒錯。」勞爾回答。

「今晚表演過後，你本來要和戴依小姐一起離開的，對嗎？」

「的確沒錯。」

「你和戴依小姐在一起，你哥哥不太開心，是吧？」

「那不關你的事。」勞爾氣憤地回答。

「你知道你哥哥的馬車原本在歌劇院外，現在卻不見了嗎？」警探詢問勞爾，「是你哥哥把戴依小姐帶走的！」

勞爾聽了很生氣，「我會找到他們。」他吼道。

勞爾離開房間後，警探笑道：「我不知道戴依小姐到底是不是伯爵帶走的，不過現在勞爾會為我們找出答案！」

p. 88–89 勞爾一衝出經理辦公室，波斯人便擋住他的去路。

「你要去哪裡？」他問勞爾。

「我要去找克莉絲汀・戴依。」勞爾回答。

「那就從歌劇院開始找起，她是從地窖離開的。」

勞爾訝異道：「你怎麼知道？」

「艾瑞克帶她走秘密通道，到他湖中的小屋去了。」波斯人平靜地說。

「你似乎對艾瑞克非常了解，你到底還知道些什麼？」勞爾問。

「他是極端危險的人物。」

「他傷過你嗎？」年輕人問他。

波斯人回答：「那一切我都已經原諒他了。」

「你和克莉絲汀都一樣，」勞爾說，「你們都認為他是個怪物，內心卻忍不住同情他。」

「噓！」波斯人要他噤聲，「他可能會聽到我們說話，現在他可能藏身在任何地方，樓層間、牆壁後面，或是天花板上。」

兩個男人來到克莉絲汀的房裡，波斯人走到鏡子前，敲了敲牆壁，突然鏡子開始旋轉。

「快來，」他對勞爾說，「我們得到地窖去，小心一點，照我所說的做。」

p. 90–91 他們走在陰暗的地窖，勞爾可以聽到老鼠跑過潮濕地板的聲音。他們兩個人不斷往前走，直到走到一面牆壁前。

「這是通往艾瑞克住處的通道，布克就是在這兒喪命的，他發現艾瑞克的住處，所以艾瑞克殺了布克，以免秘密被洩露了。」波斯人把油燈抬至牆壁上指路。

「這兒有個把手，把它拉下來門就會打開，就是這裡！」

牆壁一打開，他們便走了進去，等他們一進去，身後的門就關上了。現在他們身在一個空蕩蕩的房間裡，牆壁全都是玻璃製的。

「這是艾瑞克的酷刑室，我們得趕緊找到出路。」波斯人急迫地說道。

p. 94–95

認識故事：巴黎歌劇院裡的工作人員

在勒胡的小說推出之時，巴黎歌劇院裡的工作人員有一千五百餘人，雖然觀眾看不到大部分的工作人員，但他們都是不可或缺的，像是售票員、接待員和幫觀眾帶位的包廂管理人員。為了要能在舞台上變換布景，需要多達一百一十位的木匠，以及舞台工作人員、煤氣工人、消防員等，隨時依據指示放下布幕、點亮舞台燈火，還要確保不會發生火災意外。

另外，還有百餘位的臨時演員站在舞台後方當後景之用，這些人員通常飾演軍人或市民等人物。此外，尚有約百位芭蕾舞者和一百二十位左右的歌劇歌手在後台演唱。

畫家被僱用來維持道具完好，化妝師則讓演員在舞台上維持最佳狀態。劇院經理甚至會僱用一些人在演出的某個時間點鼓掌！每一場演出，都必須投入大量的努力與團隊合作。

[第六章] 湖中的房子

p. 96–97 就在他們在艾瑞克的酷刑室裡找出口時,波斯人對勞爾道出艾瑞克的來歷。艾瑞克過著很悲慘的日子。

「我們曾經有過好長的一段經歷。」他解釋道,「在很多年前,我們都住在波斯,在那裡工作,我是一名警察,而艾瑞克為波斯的蘇丹王工作。艾瑞克極富聰明才智,是一名出色的建築師,他為蘇丹王建造神秘的宮殿,裡面有許多秘密通道,讓蘇丹王遇到危急時可以躲藏。蘇丹還命令艾瑞克為他建一間酷刑室,他對艾瑞克聰明的創意十分著迷。」

「艾瑞克不單單是一名有創意的建築師,而且他還很會唱歌,歌聲很具感染力,到現在也還是。」波斯人繼續説。

p. 98–99 「我的確很不喜歡艾瑞克的建築作品,但對他的聰明才智與驚人的歌唱天賦,我是很敬佩的。他這一生中是幹過一些壞事,但我很同情他,人們嘲笑他,排斥他,只因為他長得很可怕。後來,波斯的蘇丹王為了不想讓他繼續去為別人效命,就想把他做掉。是我幫他逃了出來,最後他就逃到法國來了。」

「在法國,艾瑞克建造了這座歌劇院,在為蘇丹王設計秘密建築那麼多年後,什麼秘密通道啊,或是在湖面上建房子什麼的,對他而言簡直是輕而易舉的事。我一直都在注意著艾瑞克,當克莉絲汀捲入他的生活時,我很擔心。」

勞爾仔細聽著波斯人所講的事情,而此時他們仍被困在滿是鏡子的房間裡。

p. 100 突然,他們聽見牆壁的另一頭傳來了艾瑞克的聲音。「做出決定!」他喊著,「是要結婚進行曲,還是安魂曲,由妳決定,克莉絲汀。」

克莉絲汀痛苦地哭出聲,勞爾顯得焦急了起來,他多希望能從那個怪物的手中救出她。接著,他們聽到了一道溫柔的聲音。

「請不要怕我，我不是壞人，我只是要妳愛我，克莉絲汀。」

克莉絲汀並沒有回答，此時遠處傳來一陣鐘聲。

「是誰膽敢走近我的房子？」艾瑞克吼道，「我等一下再回來，克莉絲汀。」

勞爾和波斯人聽到艾瑞克離開房間的腳步聲。

p. 102–103 「如果我們對著克莉絲汀那邊叫，說不定她能過來放我們出去。」勞爾說。「克莉絲汀！克莉絲汀！」他輕輕叫著，而克莉絲汀也真的聽到了。

「勞爾，你在哪裡？」她回問道。

「我們被困在妳隔壁的房間裡，妳可以放我們出去嗎？」他問。

「我動不了，艾瑞克把我綁了起來。他說，如果我不嫁給他，他就殺光所有人，然後他再自殺，他已經瘋掉了！」她驚慌地喊著。

勞爾和波斯人明白他們現在的處境非常危險，他們到處尋找機關想把門打開。終於，波斯人找到了開關。他們打開門，走進地窖。

「這是一間酒窖。」勞爾說。

地窖裡有許許多多的大桶子。

「沒錯，不過我想這些桶子裡裝的可不是酒。」波斯人說。他打開其中一個桶子，裡面裝的全都是火藥。

「如果克莉絲汀不答應嫁給他，他打算炸掉歌劇院。」他叫道。

p. 104–105 他們立刻跑回酷刑室大吼：「克莉絲汀！」

「我還在這兒，他剛剛回來過，說那個闖入的人死了，我……我想是被他殺死的。」她驚懼地告訴他們。

「克莉絲汀，如果你不答應嫁給他，艾瑞克就要炸掉歌劇院。」勞爾對她提出警告。就在這時候,艾瑞克回來了。

「妳在跟誰說話?」他問克莉絲汀。接著他看了看酷刑室的外牆, 穿過房間敲了敲牆壁。

「勞爾來了,是不是?」他說著發出邪惡的笑聲。

克莉絲汀哀求他,「求求你讓他走!」

「那就必須由妳決定該怎麼做了!」他命令道。

「桌上有兩個盒子,一個是蚱蜢形狀的盒子,一個是蠍子的形狀,妳得轉開其中一個。要是妳選蠍子,就代表妳答應要嫁給我;選蚱蜢,就表示妳不肯嫁給我。現在就決定,克莉絲汀。」他說。

接著他便走出房門。

p. 106–107 「如果她選的是蚱蜢,地窖裡的火藥就會爆炸。」

波斯人說,他們聽到克莉絲汀在隔壁房間哭泣。

「我該怎麼做?我該怎麼做?」她哭喊著。這時艾瑞克回來了。

「好了,妳的選擇是什麼?」他問。

她轉開蠍子形狀的盒子。

這時,勞爾和波斯人聽到他們腳下傳來水流聲。

「他要用水淹沒地窖。」波斯人說。水不斷地注入地窖,接著又從地下的活板門縫灌進來。沒多久,整個房間就要被水淹沒,他們得努力找到出路活命,但很快他們倆就都失去了意識。

波斯人醒過來,發現自己躺在沙發上,艾瑞克就站在他身邊,克莉絲汀也在旁邊。

「你現在沒事了,克莉絲汀求我救你一命,我是為了她才這麼做。」艾瑞克對波斯人說。

他給波斯人喝了一點飲料,接著波斯人便沈入夢鄉。

p. 108-109 過了幾天，波斯人坐在自己公寓的沙發上，閱讀歌劇院事件的報導。勞爾哥哥的屍體在歌劇院的湖邊被發現，報紙還報導了勞爾和克莉絲汀的失蹤。

波斯人的僕人走進房裡，身後跟著一名訪客，是艾瑞克！

「你是殺人兇手！」波斯人指控艾瑞克，「為什麼要殺勞爾的哥哥？」

艾瑞克回答：「我沒有殺他，他應該是自己掉進湖裡的。我來這裡是要告訴你，這是你最後一次見我，我就快要死了。」

波斯人對這個孤獨傷心的男人一片同情。

「我已經準備好面對死亡，在我去救你和勞爾之前，她允許我親吻她，即使是我自己的母親，也從未吻過我。當我吻了克莉絲汀時，天使彷彿全都圍繞在我身邊唱歌。」艾瑞克說道。

「現在他們在哪裡？」波斯人問。

「他們很好，我送給他們一枚婚戒，祝他們永遠幸福快樂。」艾瑞克說。

波斯人可以看見艾瑞克眼中閃著淚水，而艾瑞克——這個歌劇院裡的魅影——也永遠消失了。

Answers

P. 26   **A**   **1** T   **2** F   **3** F

     B   **1** Meg's mother is the woman who is in charge of Box 5.
         2 Joseph Buquet was the man whose body was found in the cellar.
         3 He saw a head of fire which had no body.

P. 27   **C**   **1** (b)   **2** (b)

     D   **1** rushed   **2** slipped   **3** fell
         4 found   **5** was covered   **6** frightened

P. 46   **A**   **1** (a)   **2** (b)   **3** (d)

     B   **1** What happened   **2** in private
         3 outshone

P. 47   **C**   **1** F   **2** F   **3** T   **4** F   **5** T

     D   **1** had worked   **2** had never been
         3 had come   **4** had grown

P. 60   **A**   **1** - B   **2** - E   **3** - A   **4** - D   **5** - C

     B   **1** (b)   **2** (c)   **3** (a)

P. 61   **C**   **1** inn   **2** darkness   **3** grave
         4 deathly   **5** mist   **6** kneeling

P. 80   **A**   **❶** (c)   **❷** (d)   **❸** (a)

        B   **❶** (b)   **❷** (a)   **❸** (d)

P. 81   **C**   **❸** → **❶** → **❹** → **❷**

        D   **❶** even though   **❷** until   **❸** As
               ❹ when   **❺** because

P. 92   **A**   **❶** didn't he   **❷** did they   **❸** wasn't she
               ❹ have you   **❺** will they   **❻** isn't she

        B   **❷** → **❶** → **❺** → **❻** → **❸** → **❹**

P. 93   **C**   **❶** - Ⓓ   **❷** - Ⓔ   **❸** - Ⓐ   **❹** - Ⓒ   **❺** - Ⓑ

        D   **❶** T   **❷** F   **❸** T   **❹** T   **❺** F

P. 110 **A**   **❶** Raoul   **❷** Christine   **❸** Erik
               ❹ The Persian

        B   **❶** - Ⓒ   **❷** - Ⓓ   **❸** - Ⓔ   **❹** - Ⓑ   **❺** - Ⓐ

P. 111 **C**   **❶** (c)   **❷** (a)

        D   **❶** Because of my homework, I could not go to the
               movie.
               ❷ Because of the heavy traffic, I was late for
               school.
               ❸ Because of him, she improved her singing
               ability.

P. 126   **A**   **1** reliable   **2** corridor   **3** body, hanged
     4 natural suicide   **5** career   **6** scarf
     7 chest, pounding

    B   **1** Christine's singing has developed much after she fell in love. (F)

       2 The new managers of the Opera House didn't believed in the ghost. (T)

       3 Everybody hated and rejected Erik because of his appearance. (T)

       4 Erik saved Raoul because Christine promised to marry Erik. (F)

       5 Christine was surprised when she saw Erik's face, but she also felt sorry for him. (T)

P. 127   **C**   **1** Why did Christine suggest Raoul to be engaged for a month? (b)

       2 Why did Christine pretend not to know Raoul in her dressing room? (c)

    D   **1** Joseph Buquet's body was found in the cellar.

       2 Raoul went to the cellar with the Persian.

       3 Christine disappeared during the performance.

       4 Erik saved Raoul and Christine and gave them a wedding ring.

       5 People started to see strange figures in the Opera House.

       < **5** → **1** → **3** → **2** → **4** >

Adaptors

Louise Benette

Macquarie University (MA, TESOL)
Sookmyung Women's University, English Instructor

David Hwang

Michigan State University (MA, TESOL)
Ewha Womans University, English Chief Instructor,
CEO at EDITUS

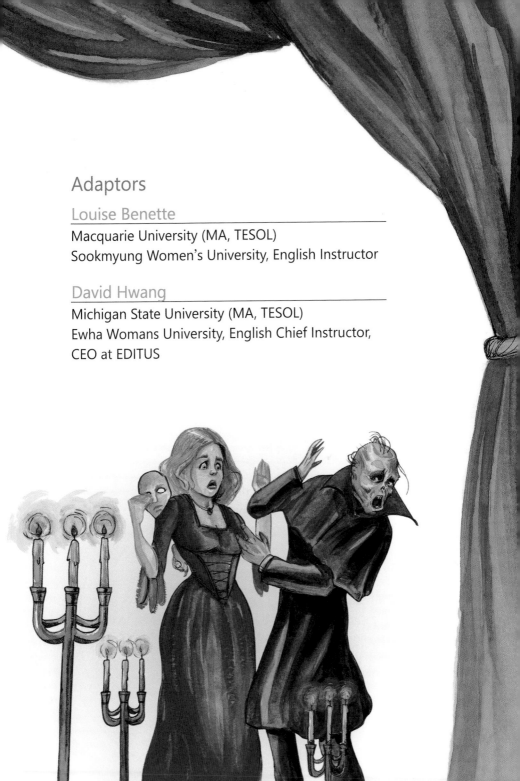

歌劇魅影【二版】
The Phantom of the Opera

作者 _ 卡斯頓‧勒胡
　　　（Gaston Leroux）

改寫 _ Louise Benette, David Hwang

插圖 _ Cristian Bernardini

翻譯 / 編輯 _ 羅竹君

作者 / 故事簡介翻譯 _ 林晨禾

校對 _ 林晨禾 / 王采翎

封面設計 _ 林書玉

排版 _ 葳豐

播音員 _ Brendan Smith, Mary Jones

製程管理 _ 洪巧玲

發行人 _ 周均亮

出版者 _ 寂天文化事業股份有限公司

電話 _ +886-2-2365-9739

傳真 _ +886-2-2365-9835

網址 _ www.icosmos.com.tw

讀者服務 _ onlineservice@icosmos.com.tw

出版日期 _ 2019年6月 二版一刷（250201）

郵撥帳號 _ 1998620-0 寂天文化事業股份有限公司

國家圖書館出版品預行編目資料

歌劇魅影【二版】/ Gaston Leroux 著；Louise
Benette, David Hwang 改寫. —二版. —[臺北市]：
寂天文化, 2019.6 面；公分. (Grade 4經典文學讀本)
譯自：The Phantom of the Opera

ISBN　978-986-318-808-7 (25K平裝附光碟片)

1. 英語　　2. 讀本

805.18　　　　　　　　　　　108008026